A SEAL TEAM
HEARTBREAKERS DUET

BREAKING TIES
&
BREAKING POINT

Teresa J. Reasor

BREAKING TIES & BREAKING POINT
A SEAL TEAM HEARTBREAKERS DUET

Contact Information: teresareasor@msn.com

Cover Art by Tracy Stewart
Edited by Faith Freewoman

Teresa J. Reasor
PO Box 124
Corbin, KY 40702

Publishing History: First Edition 2017

ISBN-13: 978-1-940047-20-1
ISBN-10: 1-940047-20-X
Print Edition

THE SEAL TEAM HEARTBREAKER NOVELLAS

BREAKING TIES: Ensign Oliver Shaker is used to making sacrifices in service to his country. Yet he's blindsided when he returns from a training rotation and learns his wife, Selena, has kept a terrible secret for weeks, as she waited for him to come home—a secret that may require a sacrifice he's not prepared to make.

Faced with a life threatening illness, Selena wants to follow the same code of strength and perseverance her husband does as a SEAL, but she can't go it alone. She needs a team, headed by her husband, to see it through. But in Oliver's line of work, duty comes first.

Still reeling from her first diagnosis, they learn Selena is pregnant. Now with two lives hanging in the balance, the emotional and physical toll stretches the ties that bind their marriage to the breaking point. But as a SEAL, Oliver never gives up. And Selena proves valor and courage don't just live on the battlefield, but in every person's heart.

BREAKING POINT: After fifteen years of marriage, Trish Marks has hit her breaking point. Her social work caseload has doubled, her son is acting out, and her SEAL husband is never home. Something has to give. When she's shot and nearly killed by an irate husband during a home check, it does.

Navy SEAL Senior Chief Petty Officer Langley Marks is five years away from retirement and his pension. He knows there's trouble in his marriage when he returns home from a deployment to a wife who's distant, overworked, stressed, and unhappy. He's only seen her like this once before, when she nearly died after giving birth to their last child. When she's shot, he re-lives that terrible experience, and feels just as helpless.

But he's not about to fly away and leave her to fight her way back alone this time. He's willing to sacrifice it all to prove to her she's the most important thing in his life. He just has to find a way to make her believe it.

TABLE OF CONTENTS

BREAKING TIES

A SEAL TEAM HEARTBREAKERS NOVELLA

Teresa J. Reasor

DEDICATION

To Joyce Brown, breast cancer survivor and Certified Breast Patient Navigator for the Baptist Healthcare Oncology Services of Corbin, Kentucky, for your help in clarifying the medical procedures needed by my character.

Any mistakes I've made are totally my own.

God bless all those brave women and men who face the battle with cancer every day with courage and humor.

And to all you ladies out there: Please do monthly exams, yearly clinical exams, and mammograms when your doctors recommend them!!

God bless our military men and women. Your sacrifices do not go unnoticed.

CHAPTER ONE

ENSIGN OLIVER 'GREENBACK' Shaker used the dense shadows to hide his position, easing into the narrow, masonry-clogged alley between two battle-scarred buildings. His body armor trapped the heat and reflected it back against his skin, and sweat poured down his back and sides like he was being sautéed inside his BDUs. He'd experienced heat before, but Iraq was surely like being trapped in the third circle of hell.

The distant sound of a baby crying came from one of the dark buildings. Through his night vision goggles he detected the dim glow of a light barely visible across the street. Some of the structures still housed families just struggling to survive while terrorist and military forces battled around them for control of the area. They had nowhere else to go, so they hunkered down and hoped the violence would pass.

What would he do if he were faced with such a terrible dilemma?

For a brief moment he allowed his thoughts to stray to Selena, waiting for him at home in San Diego. She had just sent him a short video of the doctor's most recent scan of their baby, showing how much it had grown. He'd never seen anything as beautiful as his wife's belly swollen with their child. He wanted to reach through the computer screen, to run his hands over it and feel the baby move.

He was here doing his job so no one would have to face such choices on American soil. *But, God, how he missed her!*

The civilian presence in the area was one of the reasons his team was here, risking their lives, doing this mission old-school instead of raining down ordnance.

He gripped his SCAR rifle and scanned the street for movement. It was his job to guard the team's back door, their route of escape. As soon as they finished wiring the building to blow, they'd fall back and double-time it out to wait for the structure to blow.

The first click came over his com system, signaling Hawk, his commanding officer and leader of the mission, had gained entry to the building. Next came Bowie's signal, then Doc's. Cutter's and Strong Man's clicks soon followed.

Greenback glanced at his watch and mentally marked the time. They had seven minutes to get in, set the timer and get out. Derrick Armstrong aka Strong Man would be the last man out and would set the last timer.

Greenback didn't know which was worse, being two blocks away, alone, and surrounded by insurgents. Or being inside a structure filled with explosives and occupied by terrorists. Pick a fucking card. Both sucked. But at least things had remained quiet at his...

The sound of approaching footsteps froze his thoughts and movements. He shifted, finding cover behind a jagged clump of masonry which partially blocked the alley. He waited to identify whether the person was armed or not. If he carried no weapon, Greenback would hold his position and allow the man to pass.

The baby's cry from above and across the street drew the guy's attention. He paused, the barrel of the AK-47 slung over his shoulder, pointing heavenward.

The tango was armed and on foot patrol. Possibly one of the terrorists.

The man pivoted. The glow of his flashlight swung toward the alley, reflecting off the wall opposite Greenback. Still wearing his NVGs, the light blinded him, leaving dots seared on his retinas.

Shit!

The tango shuffled into the alley. Greenback froze as the man eased past him, so close he smelled his sweat and the faint hint of garlic.

The tango halted, looking up as though he heard or sensed something. "Who is there?" he demanded in Arabic.

With the aftereffects of the flashlight still obscuring his vision, Greenback could only guess the man's location. Should the tango shout a warning to the rest of the patrol, there would be no escape for him or the team. With all his strength, Greenback swung his heavy rifle stock and connected with something solid. A hollow thump like a melon cracking open echoed through the alley. He sensed more than saw the tango's head whip back and a dull thud followed as he dropped to the ground. Greenback followed the sound, lending his weight to pinning the sentry and keeping him quiet. He gripped the man's head, the spongy feeling of crushed bones making him gag. The tango's choking struggle to breathe lasted an agonizing thirty seconds, and then his efforts ceased.

Fear and relief tangled in Greenback's gut, triggering a wave of nausea. His heart pumped hard from the surge of adrenaline, his vision slowly cleared, and he felt for a pulse. There was none. He scrambled to his feet and rolled the man against the wall.

He turned to study the street again. Had anyone heard the brief struggle? Nothing moved. How long before the next tango on patrol wandered by? There had to be more than one. What were the chances the next guy would use the alley as a shortcut? Greenback steeled himself to do whatever came next.

The baby across the street started crying again, louder and louder. Why didn't someone pick it up?

"OLIVER? OLIVER?" SELENA bounced Lucia on her hip in an attempt to soothe her. The toddler's cheeks were flushed with fever and her tiny body radiated heat. Her two-and-a-half-old daughter had never been this ill. She'd run low-grade temperatures when she was teething, and once with an ear infection, but this one was still creeping up and refused to stay down, even with children's Tylenol. Several hours later, Selena's concern had turned into full-fledged fear.

Though the room was cool, Oliver's curly, dark brown hair clung to his forehead, damp with sweat. His eyes darted back and forth beneath his lids, a sign of REM sleep. She knew better than to touch him while he was under so deeply, because he'd react like he was in danger.

His hands twitched and his breathing became uneven. What was it he dreamed about? If only he would tell her. He'd sometimes come half off the bed if she startled him awake.

"Greenback!" she said, using his SEAL handle in as commanding a tone as she could manage, since she was pretty sure he was dreaming about a mission. "Lucia is sick."

His eyes flew open and he sat up so quickly she gasped.

"What's wrong?" he asked.

Her heart flew into a wave of fast contractions, exhaustion intensifying her reaction. "Lucia's running a high fever and it's not coming down as it should, even with Tylenol. I think we need to go to the ER."

He threw back the covers and was on his feet in one smooth move. How did he go from deep sleep to wide-awake in seconds? It was a skill she could use. She was groggy from being up with the baby off and on all night. Had he not just gotten home from a training rotation she'd have asked him to help earlier. But he'd been so exhausted he'd slurred his words.

While he yanked on a pair of jeans and a T-shirt, she gently rocked Lucia and bathed her face with a cool cloth. Instead of soothing her, the damp rag seemed to make her scream louder.

"Let me take her, so you can get dressed." Oliver plucked Lucia from her arms and cuddled her close while he did the dance and dip movement that usually rocked her to sleep. His dark hair, so much like the baby's, clung in ringlets where he'd splashed water to smooth it down.

"Daddy-daddy-daddy." Lucia strung the syllables together in a monotonous chant while Selena got dressed, but at least she was no longer screaming.

Selena hurried into a pair of jeans and a blouse and stuffed her feet into slip-on tennis shoes. She dragged her long hair into a scrunchie to pull it back from her face.

Oliver frowned, his concern clear in his brow and compressed lips. "Jesus, she really is hot. Why didn't you wake me sooner?"

Defensive and worried, she said, "I gave her some children's Tylenol, thinking it would bring the fever down until I could take her into the pediatrician's office this morning. It obviously didn't work."

She gathered the diaper bag and her purse. Oliver carried Lucia, followed her to the van parked alongside their small house, opened the back door, and secured Lucia in her car seat.

"I'll sit back here with her while you drive," Selena said, climbing in next to the baby seat. She fished in her bag and found the keys and handed them to him.

"Daddy-daddy-daddy."

"Daddy's driving, baby. We'll be there in a minute," Oliver said while he quickly backed the vehicle out of the driveway.

Of course Lucia would want Oliver. She'd had a steady diet of Mama for the last six weeks. Tears blurred Selena's eyes at her unexpected resentment. He swung through just long enough for her and Lucia to rain their affections on him, then he swooped back out again.

She snapped the seat belt on and laid a soothing hand on Lucia's chest as she began to struggle against the restraints of the car seat and cry.

Lucia had been more fussy than usual for the last few days. And her nose had run a little. Selena scolded herself for not noticing sooner, but it was so hard being responsible for everything on top of her work at the bank. The house, the yard, the van, Lucia. *Everything*.

Being married to a SEAL was like being single nine months out of the year, with no companionship and no sex. As much as she'd wanted a family, she hadn't realized she'd be raising Lucia mostly on her own.

She'd kept everything together until last Friday, though. But now fear cramped her stomach. Every time she thought about it, a gut-clenching dread swamped her.

She needed to tell Oliver. And she would. As soon as Lucia was better. She couldn't worry about it while her baby was ill.

Oliver looked up into the rear view mirror at her. "How long has she been sick?"

"Just this evening. She's been a little fussy the last few days, but nothing I could put my finger on."

He turned into the Balboa Medical Center parking lot. "I'll drop you at the ER entrance and go park the van. I'll be back as soon as I can."

"Okay," Selena murmured, already busy releasing Lucia from the car seat. Selena lifted her free and grabbed her purse and the diaper bag from the floor. As soon he stopped the van, she got out and shoved the door closed. He drove away immediately.

While Selena sat in a small privacy cubicle and provided the woman checking them in with all the necessary information, Lucia clung to her and cried. The sound bounced off the sides of the small space, magnifying it. With each second, the tension headache pounding at the nape of Selena's neck intensified.

Finally Oliver appeared at the mouth of the cubicle. His hair, now dry, lay in heavy curls, accentuating his olive-skinned Italian good looks. The girl behind the computer flashed him a smile and sat up straighter. He nodded to her. His biceps flexed against the short sleeves of his T-shirt as he lifted Lucia. "I'll see if I can entertain her until we're called back into an examination room."

Selena watched his progress down the hall to the waiting room. Carrying forty to sixty pounds of gear during every mission, and the constant physical training he and the team did, had honed his five-eight frame into muscular perfection. Her desire for him had never waned. All he had to do was look at her with his heavy-lidded, chocolate brown eyes, and she was hot for him. And he reacted the same way to her. Would he still feel that way after she told him?

She collected her insurance card and identification from the girl and walked back to join Oliver and Lucia in the waiting area. Four other people waited ahead of them.

Since Lucia seemed to prefer the hall to the waiting area, Oliver walked her up and down, doing his dance, bounce move. Her throat closed just watching him. Loving him and Lucia was the one thing keeping her together, keeping her strong. But she didn't feel strong right now. She felt shaky and afraid. Afraid for herself, but afraid for Lucia and Oliver, too.

The waiting area cleared out quickly, and a nurse called them back to the examination room. The claustrophobic closeness of the space was stifling, and she struggled to push the air in and out.

"You okay, hon?" Oliver asked, a frown working its way across his face.

Lucia reached for her, giving her an excuse to focus on their child instead of the walls closing in around her. "I'm fine." She cuddled her daughter close and grabbed a tissue to wipe Lucia's nose. The doctor came in before Oliver could probe any further.

Lucia screamed at having a strange man touch her. Selena answered the doctor's questions while Oliver held the toddler during the examination. At his diagnosis of another ear infection, Selena frowned in concern. "She just got over an ear infection last month."

"Do you know if she has any allergies?" he asked.

"No."

He studied the chart. "How often have the infections reoccurred?"

"Just in the last four months she's had three."

"Is she in daycare?"

"Five days a week, while I'm at work."

"Children in daycare are more susceptible to bacterial infections. Children indiscriminately spread germs. Any pets?"

"No."

"Any stuffed toys she sleeps with?"

"Her lamb."

"I'd recommend washing it as often as possible, or slipping it out of her bed once she's asleep. Toys harbor bacteria.

"With children this age," the doctor continued, "the Eustachian tubes are flatter and narrow. They don't drain as easily as adults. That allows bacteria to build up and causes fluid to gather behind the eardrum and cause the pain.

"It's too soon to tell, though, because that last infection might not have responded to the first antibiotic she took, and it lingered. I'll give her something a little stronger and see if we can't wipe it out. But if she continues to develop them, your regular pediatrician may want her to see an ear, nose, and throat specialist. If she doesn't respond to the antibiotic quickly, take her in to see your regular doctor immediately."

"Thank you. I will."

Half an hour later they were out of the ER, with prescriptions for some drops to numb Lucia's pain and the antibiotic.

Although they rushed through an all-night pharmacy and picked up the prescription, the sky was already lightening as they reached home. Selena gave Lucia, now exhausted from crying, a dose of the antibiotic. Oliver administered the ear drops and got the baby down while Selena made coffee.

Their small, bungalow-style house had been a labor of love. They remodeled things when they could afford to, and the kitchen had been their first project together. The terracotta tile floors glowed with warmth. They'd painted the cabinets a pale sky blue and distressed them. The glass doors shone. Fresh herbs filled the room with fragrances from a window box garden in the small breakfast nook next to the round kitchen table. Selena stacked the bills and letters spread across the table and set them aside. She settled there while she waited for the coffee to brew and for Oliver to join her.

Though exhaustion dragged at her limbs and she longed for sleep, they needed to talk. She needed to tell him, though the dread of it made her want to throw up. Just saying the words would make things real for her, for them both. And change things for them—between them—forever.

Ten minutes later, Oliver wandered into the room and paused

at the coffee maker to pour them each a cup. He added cream to hers, then sauntered over to the table. The deliberate way he placed his feet, the measured distance between steps, was a SEAL thing, perpetuated by their training. She would recognize him in a crowd of a thousand other men just by the way he walked.

He slid the cup in front of her. "Are you sure you want to drink coffee? Since you've been up with the baby all night, I can hold down the fort while you sleep."

"I may in a bit." She concentrated on the cup in front of her to keep from tearing up. "There's something I have to tell you. I couldn't while you were on your training rotation, but now you're home—"

Oliver frowned and placed a hand over the one she clenched on the kitchen table. "What is it?"

She studied his features…so strong, so masculine. She'd seen him smiling like a fool all the way through their wedding. Seen him grimace in release when they made love. Seen him luminous with pride and joy when he'd first set eyes on Lucia when he'd come home from a deployment. What would his expression reveal when she told him?

She swallowed. "Three weeks ago I found a lump in my breast and went to the doctor. I may have cancer."

CHAPTER TWO

WHILE SELENA TOOK a shower, Oliver sat at the kitchen table. He stared rigidly at his clenched fists. He wanted to pound on something. Pound it until his fists were bloody. Anything to rid himself of the gut-wrenching fear. If he lost it, it would frighten Selena and wake the baby. He forced his fingers to relax and pressed his hands flat on the tabletop.

While he'd been having a blast practicing defensive driving skills, she'd learned she might have cancer. She'd had to deal with the aftermath of hearing those words *alone*.

Guilt crashed into him with the punch of a breaching ram. The black coffee in his stomach burned like battery acid. *Sweet Jesus.* Nausea rolled over him.

He couldn't catch his breath. He ran five miles a day. Hit the weight and exercise equipment three times a week. Did PT when he needed it and, in certain instances, just to pass the time. But sitting across the table from his wife and hearing those words had punched the air out of him. Though he'd held her, told her everything was going to be okay, he hadn't recovered. Not yet. He hadn't drawn a full breath—and probably wouldn't until the results from the needle biopsy were in—and only then if he knew for certain she didn't have cancer.

She couldn't have cancer. *Please, God, don't let Selena have cancer.*

He shot up from the table and strode down the hall to Lucia's bedroom. The combination of medication and exhaustion had finally overtaken the toddler, and she'd fallen asleep, her tiny limbs sprawled in boneless abandon, her hands curled into loose fists. Even in sleep she was taking on the world. Which was when his daughter was most like him. When awake and well she was never still, never quiet. She hustled through her day like she wanted to discover and absorb everything she could in as little time as possible.

If Selena was sick, how would she be able to keep up with Lucia?

At the sound of the water being turned off, Oliver left Lucia's room and wandered into their bedroom. He hadn't done enough to comfort his wife, to bolster her courage. How could he accomplish it? What could he do to show his support?

Selena opened the bathroom door. Her dark hair was bound in a towel, her body wrapped in a long terrycloth robe. He had seen her that way—all bundled up in robe and turban after a shower—a million times, and never felt closed off from her. But something in her posture, her expression, warned him to keep his distance this time.

The first time they'd made love had been after a trip to the beach. She had just showered off the sand and salt, and had worn a similar robe, with a bright red towel wrapped turban-style around her hair. He had led her over to sit on the bed, loosened the heavy weight of her wet hair, and buried his fingers in it. He'd cradled her face in his hands and kissed her until she opened her lips to him, and then her body.

"What can I do, Selena?" he asked, his voice husky, echoing his emotions.

"Nothing." Her voice had an edge to it, then softened. "I'm tired. I've been up all night with Lucia. I just need to sleep."

"We both do." He kicked off his shoes and stripped off the brown T-shirt and cammies. In his boxer briefs he stretched out on the bed. When she climbed into bed, he'd hold her.

She went to the dresser, tossed the wet towel in the hamper next to it and reached for her brush. She brought it with her to the bed and, sitting on the edge, ran the bristles through her hair, her movements sluggish with exhaustion.

Her glorious mass of hair had a life of its own. Even wet, it lay in heavy waves down her back and across her shoulders. Would chemotherapy strip her luxuriant symbol of vitality away and kill it while it killed the cancer?

How would she deal with it? How would he?

A new wave of anxiety struck him. He needed to hold her. "Come to bed, Selena. Lucia will be back up before you have time to close your eyes."

She set aside the brush and lay upon the cover, but turned her back to him.

Fuck that. Never in their married life had there been any kind of emotional distance between them. Even when a bit of resentment lingered following an argument, they reached for each other. He wasn't letting this take hold. Not now. He looped an arm around her waist and tugged her back against him to spoon.

A tense silence stretched between them, until she guided his hand beneath her robe and held it cupped around her bare breast. Relief flooded him, and he drew his first full breath since she'd said the C word. Her skin was silky smooth, warm, inviting beneath his palm. She had beautiful breasts, full, round, more than his hand could hold, but not so much she looked out of proportion. Instead of sex, his thoughts turned to the way Selena had nestled Lucia against her and offered the baby her nipple for the first time. Selena's face had literally glowed with love and purpose while Lucia latched on and nursed.

Selena turned, her shoulder pushed against his chest and her tear-glazed eyes, bruised with pain, raised to his. "I'm scared, Oliver," she whispered.

Though her tone was soft, it might as well have been a shout. He could protect her from terrorists and other bad things in the world, but he couldn't do a damn thing to shield her from this. The raw emotion on her face, her tear-filled eyes, intensified his helplessness. He tried to swallow but his mouth was dry. "I am, too, *tesoro*." His fingers lingered around her breast in a soothing caress. "We need to stay calm until we know what we're dealing with. Then we'll decide on a plan. And if it is breast cancer…well, the docs cure it every day." *Didn't they?* "It's going to be okay."

It had to be.

He would not accept any other outcome.

SELENA WOKE WITH a start, her heart racing. What happened? Had she heard something? Had she forgotten something?

The house lay quiet around her. The bedside clock read 11:35, its ticking as loud as the rhythmic hammer of drumsticks beating time.

Fear surged over her, bringing with it the reason behind her roiling gut and panicky heartbeat. It was as if her survival mode was stuck in first gear, already at full throttle every time her eyes opened. She wanted to run, but where? Where could she go and not hear a constant replay of the words, "I think we need to do a biopsy."

Silence closed in around her, making her thoughts too strident to bear. She rolled off the bed and shuffled down the hall to Lucia's room. Her daughter's yellow comforter with purple butterflies was smoothed over the bed, and the stuffed lamb she slept with lay propped against the pillows. The clothes basket, usually filled with clean clothes waiting to be folded, sat empty.

Selena wandered on to the living room. The toys Lucia kept scattered around the room had been tossed into the wooden box behind the sofa, and the room was straightened.

She needed a cup of coffee and some aspirin to offset the hungover feeling from sleeping too long. The kitchen looked as clean as the other rooms, and even the few dirty dishes left in the sink earlier had been washed and left to dry in the drainer.

Though she should have been grateful Oliver had worked so hard to clean up the messes left behind by an active toddler, she wasn't. She had hours to fill and nothing to fill them with. Nothing to keep her mind off of the lump in her breast. She clenched her hand at her side to keep from touching the spot, now tender from being examined, stuck by a needle and probed by her own compulsive fingertips. Every time she touched it she prayed it would be gone. It had to be some awful mistake.

She set up the coffee pot and, finding a bottle of aspirin in the kitchen cabinet, took two. She sat down at the table and noticed the note propped against the small ceramic pot kept on the windowsill over the sink. They used it to store small odds and ends—paperclips, pencils, rubber bands, screws—anything which might be a choking hazard for a busy, curious, two-and-a-half-year-old girl.

Selena wandered over and retrieved the note. Oliver's square, masculine script said, *Don't cook. Lucia and I have gone out to get a late lunch. Be back in thirty minutes.* The time on the note was 11:15.

She'd spent fifteen minutes walking through the house and making coffee. She needed to get dressed. She would not allow herself to lie around in a depressed funk. She wouldn't allow Oliver to see her like this...or Lucia. She had to get on with the business of living.

Everyone died. What counted was how you spent the time you had.

Oliver faced death every time he went into battle. He'd done it again and again every time he'd been downrange in the six years he'd been a SEAL. She could at least face this small lump in her breast with as much courage as he faced his duty.

She shoved her fingers though her tangled hair and squeezed her throbbing temples. Telling herself these things and living them were two different things.

But she *had* to do this. She had no other choice.

Bringing the cup of coffee to fortify her, Selena went into the bathroom. She grimaced at her reflection. Her hair was a wild snarl and her face puffy from sleep. She ran a cool basin of water and bathed her face, tamed her hair by pulling it back into a ponytail, brushed her teeth, and put on a light smattering of makeup.

By the time she heard a car pull up outside, she was dressed in white capris, a top with tiny flowers printed on it and slip-on tennis shoes. She met Oliver at the door with a smile and held it open for him.

Oliver brushed a kiss against her cheek as he shouldered past her with bags of Chinese food in both hands. "Lucia's right behind me. Her fever's down, the drops are working and I think the antibiotic has kicked in."

Lucia climbed the two steps up on the small porch by clinging to the railing. She greeted Selena with, "I want eggroll."

"I hope daddy got eggroll." Selena stepped out on the porch to help her up the last step into the house.

"Daddy got six eggrolls," Oliver said from the kitchen.

Lucia laughed. "You're funny Daddy."

Just hearing her speak in a sentence instead of the daddy-daddy-daddy mantra she'd done at the hospital was a relief.

By the time she had lifted Lucia onto her booster seat at the table, Oliver had placed an egg roll, fried rice and some sweet and sour chicken, chopped in small pieces, on a plastic plate. He set it in front of Lucia, and she dug in with her spoon.

"Are you feeling better?" he asked as they sat down at the table together.

"Yes. I got some sleep and I'm better."

She turned to brush a dark curl back behind Lucia's ear to keep her from getting food in it. "I noticed how you and daddy cleaned up the living room and your room. You both did a good job."

"Toys go in the box."

"Yes, you're right. When you're not playing with them, toys go in the box."

Lucia nodded adamantly. She gripped her egg roll in a tiny fist and gnawed on one end.

"I'm always surprised she likes cabbage," Oliver said.

"She'll actually eat anything you or I do. And I'm glad to see her appetite's back. She's been a little finicky the last few days. I should have realized something was brewing."

Oliver paused, his fork midway to his mouth. "Selena—you're

already a super mom. To catch every nuance, you'd have to be psychic."

She nodded. Hearing him say it did help a little. Silence fell between them and she concentrated on her food.

"When will we know?" he asked.

"Tomorrow or the next day."

He nodded. "After we eat, let's go for a drive. We can stop somewhere for dinner."

"Okay." She understood his need for action. If you kept on the move, time passed more quickly. For the last two weeks, she'd been in a state of hyperactivity, rushing from one thing to the next.

She was relieved to have a task to complete. She packed a tote bag for Lucia, storing the medicine in a small cooling bag, then added extra clothes, wipes, drinks, snacks, and toys. Once they were in the car with Lucia secured in her car seat in the back, Oliver pointed the van north.

"Where are we going?" she asked.

"Laguna Beach. I thought we'd walk the beach. Maybe go to the museum if it's still open when we're through."

"We can eat at Las Brisas next door," she suggested. "We haven't been in a long time."

"Sounds good."

Silence lingered. Oliver rolled down the windows so the breeze blew through, bringing with it the rush of the wind and scent of the sea. Traffic was light, but the drive to Laguna would take anywhere between two and three hours, depending on the traffic. By midway Lucia grew restless, so Oliver pulled over at Oceanside and they all got out to stretch their legs.

The breeze off the water was chilly, so Selena bundled Lucia into the sweater and hat she'd packed earlier. They walked down the long stretch of concrete sidewalk, both of them holding Lucia by a hand while Oliver pushed the empty umbrella stroller.

They reached the pier, and Selena experienced a twinge while she strapped Lucia into the stroller. She was a petite child, in the bottom twenty-five percent for height and weight, understandable since neither of her parents were big people. But she had almost outgrown the small, portable stroller. Her baby had become a toddler overnight. Where had the time gone? She wanted to roll it all back and relive every moment with more clarity, more attention.

Her eyes blurred with tears, and she shoved her sunglasses on and turned to look out to sea so Oliver wouldn't know. Cirrus clouds shaped like ostrich feathers fluttered across a clear blue sky. The Pacific Ocean stretched to the horizon, its color darkened to ultramarine.

Her gaze settled on her husband while he pushed the stroller and pointed out things to Lucia. Though he only stood five foot eight, he was muscular and fit. Because of his broad shoulders and back, he always seemed taller, and bigger than his one hundred sixty-five pounds. His movements were relaxed, but every step he took radiated purpose and drive.

Should something happen to her, he'd grieve, but he'd move on. He'd formulate a plan to fulfill Lucia's needs and see it through. He'd make sure their daughter was cared for and loved.

Just as she would have to, should anything happen to him.

But would he sacrifice his calling, his job, for Lucia? And who would he find to care for her while he was out of the country, as he often was?

Gulls screeched overhead and Lucia pointed upward as she followed their flight. As though sensing Selena's absence, Oliver stopped and looked over his shoulder, searching for her. She hurried to catch up.

"You, okay, *cara*?" he asked.

She nodded. "Yes. Just admiring the scenery."

Another couple, pushing a double stroller with twins strapped in it, strolled by and exchanged a smile and a nod with Selena.

She experienced another wave of anxiety. If she took chemo for a long time, she'd never be able to have another child. She'd be sterile.

She and Oliver planned to have another baby, had been semi-trying for the last six months, in between his training rotations.

Their dreams of another child would end.

"Have you called your mom to talk about any of this?" Oliver asked.

"No, I didn't want to worry them until I knew something for certain. Maybe not even then."

"Your mom and sisters will be hurt if you don't tell them, Selena."

"Not yet, Oliver." Every time she said the C word it made it more real, more certain. If she told her family, they'd call her constantly. Their questions and good intentions would undermine what little control she had over her fear. She had to get a handle on everything before she spoke to them.

"You haven't told anyone?"

"I told you."

His dark eyes searched her face, then he slipped an arm around her and rested his lips against her forehead. She wrapped her arms around him and held on. Her anxiety eased.

"Go, Daddy." Lucia's voice, impatient and demanding, interrupted the moment. She rocked back and forth as though she could move the stroller with her will alone. Oliver grabbed the handles and pushed her along again while they continued up the pier.

CHAPTER THREE

SELENA'S FRENETIC UNLOADING of their laundry basket of beach paraphernalia convinced Oliver she was on the brink of implosion. One minute she threw herself into an activity, the next she dropped so deep into her thoughts he feared she'd never surface. How long had she been like this?

The thing was, he felt the same way...and he didn't like it one damn bit. He was used to action, but there wasn't a damn thing to do right now but wait. The waiting he did as a SEAL was long and boring, sometimes fraught with danger, but at least they saw an end to it. He couldn't see an end this time. There were too many unknowns. The tight band around his chest was suddenly unbearable.

There were only a few clusters of people on the beach, and the tide would be in soon. He decided to let Selena finish unloading and led Lucia by the hand to a tide pool tucked in an outcropping of rock at one end of the cove. The water was rising, and he was surprised when the toddler ignored the splash of the breakers and concentrated on settling her small feet on the slick rocks.

She squatted down eagerly when they arrived at the pool. Starfish and sea anemones of a variety of colors clung to the pitted surface, and small fish wove their way between them in the shallow water. A hermit crab scuttled between two submerged rocks and paused to feed on the brown algae coating the shallow pools.

"Peach," Lucia declared, squatting and pointing at a sea star.

Oliver shook his head. "It's a starfish, baby."

"Peach."

"Peach is a character in her current favorite cartoon," Selena explained from behind them.

"I'm relieved." He was also relieved she'd decided to join them. "I was trying to figure out how to set her straight."

"The story also has a shrimp in it. I fixed shrimp one night for supper and she cried for an hour. It took me half an hour to figure out what she was upset about. I explained that Jacque, the shrimp character, was not on her plate, and then she was fine."

Oliver chuckled.

They tiptoed around a mussel bed and spied a small octopus clinging to the rocks.

"Look at this little guy, Lucia. Isn't he something? He's an octopus." He spent several moments getting her to say the word and finally settled for ocpus. "Our girl is really smart," he said over his shoulder.

"Yes, she is."

After a few more minutes of exploration, he lifted Lucia on his shoulders and carried her back to the strip of beach where her toys waited. Lucia ran to her bulldozer and began making motor noises while she pushed sand around with the vehicle's toy scoop.

Selena said, "I can't make up my mind whether she's going to be a construction worker or an engineer." She sat on the blanket, stretched out her legs, and crossed her ankles.

"Let's hope an engineer." Oliver sat beside her. "She'll be doing something creative and earning good money."

Selena smiled. "You know you'd have just as much pride in her no matter what she does."

He would. His baby girl was his angel. "As long as she's happy. Speaking of happy, how are plans going for Brett and Tess's wedding?"

"Tess gets together with me and the other wives once every

couple of weeks for dinner. We talk about the progress and brainstorm for places she can call to get things done. She's pretty much arranged most of the wedding, since Brett went wheels up right after he'd popped the question. We even went along while she shopped for her wedding gown. It's beautiful. She's beautiful."

"Not as beautiful as you, *cara mia*. I still remember how you looked on our wedding day." He caught the flash of doubt in her eyes. "I do. You had tiny pink roses in your bouquet and in your hair. And your dress had a rose pattern in the lace. I kept thinking you'd decide at the last minute you didn't want to take a chance on a guy who wasn't even out of college. Especially one who had plans to go into the Navy as soon as he graduated."

"I can't believe you remember the lace on my dress. We were so young and fearless back then." She smiled, and for once no melancholy lurked beneath her expression. "Do you think Brett will make it back in time?"

Oliver shrugged. "There's no guarantee. He had to fill out the paperwork to notify HQ and his commanding officer of his intent to marry. If he's not in the thick of things, he'll make it."

"I don't know what she'll do if he doesn't get back."

"They can always Skype the ceremony and have a private one once he's home."

Her eyes rounded in amazement. "Ohmygod! Skype the ceremony? Would it even be a legal marriage?"

"Well, not if he isn't here to sign the marriage license. I think in the state of California you both have to be present during the ceremony. But he'd be there to say his vows and the I do's, so she wouldn't have to cancel the whole thing.

"Oliver, you have no romance in your soul. Skype the ceremony!" She shot him an exasperated *men!* look.

He grinned at her. "We'll see how much romance I have once we get back home tonight."

Her eyes widened.

He covered her hand with his. "You have to live each moment as it comes, *cara*. You can't let this take you out of the fight."

Selena remained silent for a moment. "Is that how you think, feel, when you're—doing what you do?"

"Yeah. And I do whatever I have to so I can come home to you and Lucia."

Her fingers tightened around his. Her eyes glazed with tears.

"My job is my job, Selena and it's important. But you and Lucia are my world."

She looked out to sea. "Do you think it's any different for me?"

He frowned, his throat tight with emotion. "No. I know it's the same."

The continued to hold hands while their daughter played.

Meantime, the tide crept closer to the blanket and to Lucia's small section of beach.

Selena seemed calmer now. "Is Lucia hungry yet?" Oliver asked, loud enough for his daughter to hear.

"Yes!" She struggled to her feet, covered in sand with the bulldozer in hand.

Oliver grimaced. "We need a built-in shower for the van. I picked the only beach in Laguna without a bathroom."

"No worries. I brought fresh clothing. We never leave home without at least three outfits."

Selena did so many things he'd never noticed. He needed to start paying attention in case he had to help out later.

THEY ATE AT Las Brisas as she'd suggested. The popular restaurant was crowded and noisy and made up for the quiet at their table. They shared a bit of the food from both their plates with Lucia, and she surprised them both by eating guacamole.

On the way home Lucia valiantly fought sleep as she watched a cartoon on the iPad Selena kept in her bag. As her eyes closed, it slid from her grasp to balance precariously on her lap. Selena caught it before it could hit the floor and unplugged the earphones.

Oliver's words earlier at the beach replayed in her mind. He was right, she owed it to him, and to Lucia, to embrace her life the best she could. She was alive right now. Not dying. She tilted her head back and watched the light fade from the horizon and turn to a velvety purple. She had to find her way around the fear and move on.

When Oliver pulled into their driveway and parked, he said, "I'll get Lucia if you can get the bag with her medicine. I'll unload the other stuff in the morning."

"Okay." Selena got out and opened the side door to get the tote bag she'd stored behind the seat, then stepped back so Oliver could get Lucia. She lay limp against Oliver's shoulder, deeply asleep. Selena eased the van door closed and hurried to open the front door, then lock it behind them. She followed Oliver down the hall to Lucia's room and folded down the comforter and sheet so he could slide her into bed.

Selena eased Lucia's sneakers off, then her socks, and brushed the sand from her feet before tucking them beneath the sheet. A bath and clean sheets would be the first order of business in the morning.

Oliver drew the sheet and comforter up over the sleeping toddler and leaned down to brush his lips against her cheek.

He straightened and breathed against Selena's ear, "I'm going to take a shower. Want to join me?"

She turned to look up at him, and he kissed her. Warm and soft, his lips moved against hers, tempting her to lean into him and increase the pressure.

He was her light, her world, just as he said she and Lucia were his. She needed to be close to him. He made her feel stronger.

She ran her hands up under his T-shirt and caressed the flat planes of his shoulder blades as she nestled in close and felt the immediate response of his body to hers. Would he still react the same way if they took her breast?

Desperation took hold and she tugged her hands free of his shirt, encircled his neck with her arms. She needed to forget everything but them for a little while. She broke the kiss. "How about that shower?"

Oliver took her hand and pulled her toward their bedroom.

AS THE ONLY child of an Irish American father with Native American roots and an Italian mother, Oliver had believed he knew all about love until he met Selena. She had been shy at first, but seductive at the same time. He'd wondered about those mixed signals until he figured out she was as inexperienced as he was about real passion, and neither of them had any idea how to handle the fact that they couldn't keep their hands off of each other. All they had to do was be in the same room for it to combust. It had taken them by storm, and they married before either of them graduated.

She loved with the hot, passionate nature of her Mediterranean heritage. In the shower, the brush of her soapy hand along his rib cage, the sweet scrape of her teeth against his shoulder, made every nerve sing. His cock hardened, and when her hand encircled it, running up and down its length, he thought he might explode.

"My turn, *cara mia.*"

He turned so the shower spray would stream over his shoulder and down between them. He filled his hand with body wash and guided her to turn so she could lean back against him. He soaped her throat, her shoulders, careful not to put any pressure on her breasts. He wanted to give her pleasure, but to feel the lump himself would destroy him. Instead he cupped the underside of both and kneaded them, then toyed with her nipples.

Her bottom moved back against him, his erection sliding between the cheeks of her ass while her hands gripped the outside of his thighs. Looking down on her soapy, water-slick breasts, Oliver had to count backwards from twenty-five to keep from going off right then.

When he was certain of his control, he pumped more bath wash into his hand and continued down the slope of her ribs to her belly. He nipped the smooth skin of her shoulder and tasted the water and the lingering essence of the soap as he caressed her upper thighs, then moved inward till his fingers found the moist heat between her legs.

Selena braced a foot on the edge of the tub, giving him complete access as she moved beneath his touch. Her throaty groan echoed against tile and tub while he caressed the tiny, sensitive nub of flesh at the top of her nether lips, then slid a finger into her. Her channel felt hot, and the ripple of her body drew it in further.

It was his groan that bounced around the shower then. He needed to be inside her. Resting a hand against her belly he dragged her back beneath the spray and let the water run down their bodies and rinse the soap away.

He stepped out of the shower and, grabbing a towel, offered her a hand. He looped the towel around her hips and, walking backward, guided her toward the bed.

"We've left the water on," she said, her voice breathy and soft.

"I'll get it later."

"We're still wet."

"So?"

They fell upon the bed together, and, for the first time since he'd arrived home, Selena laughed. The sound, throaty and hoarse, was the biggest seduction of all. He loved her laugh. He kissed her and she hooked a leg over his hip, urging him on. He rolled between her thighs and gave them both what they wanted. The sweet, moist heat of her welcomed him, and he stilled, savoring the sensation as their bodies meshed. "I love you, Selena."

"Per l'eternità?" For all time?

"Per l'eternità," he agreed.

"Then I am whole."

Forever. He moved, filling her, then drawing almost free, and her hands gripped his hips. Her body tensed and pulsed, bearing down on him, then opening for his next thrust. This erotic dance they had performed for eight years together had never seemed more intense, more passionate. Her hand slid between them to cup his balls, and her thumb rested at the base of his erection, putting more upward pressure on his thrusts, giving them both more pleasure.

She murmured his name, her voice breaking with emotion. Her hips rolled and she contracted around him as she found what she sought, so he buried himself in her and welcomed his own release.

Though he'd never before been emotional during sex, tears clouded his vision now, and he turned his face into the strands of wet hair curling across her pillow. *Per l'eternità.*

CHAPTER FOUR

SELENA KEPT A tight grip on her purse strap. She rarely carried more than a small clutch, but today needed something more substantial to cling to. She scanned the waiting room one more time, for lack of anything else to do, but the landscape hadn't changed in the past five minutes. Women sat around the room in various postures and stages of pregnancy, along with women like her waiting to see the doctor for other reasons.

Like all doctors' waiting rooms, the patients spoke in subdued tones, but there were laughter and smiles as well. *How far along are you? Don't you just hate it when your feet swell?* All the discomfort and joy of pregnancy was bounced back and forth, though the women were often strangers. A young woman sat two seats down from them, her baby, tiny, carefully swaddled in a carrier/car seat. She was probably there for her two-week checkup.

Oliver sat beside her and, though he held a *National Geographic,* and his eyes rested on a page, but he hadn't turned it. In fact, if his eyes had not been open, she'd have sworn he was taking one of his power naps. Men were always uncomfortable in a gynecologist's office, but was he experiencing the same heart-sickening fear and pain she was?

An older woman, maybe in her early fifties, entered the office, checked in at the window and sat down near the door. A brightly colored scarf, pulled tight around her head, followed the round curve of her skull and ended in a long tail down her back.

Selena fought the urge to brush back a long strand of her thick, dark hair for fear the woman would notice.

Would she lose her hair, too? Of course she would.

Her heart raced, harsh and sickening. Nausea surged up to coat her mouth with saliva. Sweat pooled beneath her arms and between her breasts.

A nurse came to the door leading back into the examining rooms and Selena's head jerked up along with everyone else's. The nurse's eyes came to rest on her, "Selena."

Oliver reached for her arm. Her legs shook as she stood.

"Doctor Sanderlin will see you in her office now." The nurse led the way past a number of examination rooms and turned two corners before they arrived at a door. The black plate fastened to it at eye level read Captain Alicia Sanderlin M.D. ObGyn. After a brief tap the nurse opened the door and motioned them in. "Please have a seat, Dr. Sanderlin will be with you in a moment."

A large cherry wood desk and desk chair dominated the room, its surface cluttered with paperwork. A bud vase with three pink roses, some baby's-breath, and greenery sat on one corner. Behind it a bookcase stretched, filled with medical texts and decorative knickknacks. Three well-stuffed armchairs upholstered in a rich burgundy fabric sat in front of the desk in a curve. Striped drapes matched their color and the gray carpet.

They'd barely sat down when Dr. Sanderlin rushed in. Oliver stood politely while Selena shoved to her feet.

"I'm sorry you had to wait, Ensign Shaker, Selena." She paused to shake Oliver's hand, then retrieved a file from her desk, and, instead of sitting behind it, she repositioned the third chair so she could face them both.

Her gaze moved from Oliver to Selena and stayed there. The woman had been her ObGyn since they'd moved to San Diego, and Selena trusted her to be both caring and a straight shooter. But God, she wanted to be anywhere else but sitting in front of her in this chair now.

"I have some good news and some not so good news," she

said, her pale green eyes steady. "Mixed in with all the other tests we ran last week, we did a pregnancy test, and it came back positive."

Selena caught her breath and her hand instinctively curved around her lower abdomen. Oh, God, what would this mean if she was sick? "I'm a little late, but I thought it was probably because of…of…everything else."

"Well, from your HCG levels, I'd say you're between six and seven weeks pregnant. Before you leave today we'll do a preliminary exam and try and pin it down."

Selena reached out to Oliver, and he took her hand and squeezed it, but his open joy when he'd gotten the news about Lucia was absent, as it was for her. The worry overshadowed everything else. How were they supposed to feel about this?

Dr. Sanderlin drew a deep breath. "Now for the not so good news." She opened the file. "The surgical oncologist we referred you to submitted this pathology report to me. I want to go over everything with you both in depth."

Selena nodded, unable to speak.

"The tissue sample did show a malignancy."

Oliver's fingers squeezed hers almost to the point of pain, then eased off.

Selena curled the fingers of her other hand against her throat as bile rose again.

"From the position of the tumor, we believe it is Ductal Carcinoma. An HER2 test was done. This test detects the proteins in the cancer cells which tell the cells to grow and divide. It came back negative, which is a very good thing. We also tested the tissue to see if it was hormone-receptor negative or positive. It is positive for hormone receptors."

Dr. Sanderlin slid closer to the edge of her seat. "With this type of cancer, the tumor feeds off the estrogen in your system. But, based on the numerous ultrasound images we did, it's fairly small, so we'll be able to tell if it's spread beyond the boundaries of the initial tumor when it's surgically removed and a dissection of your lymph nodes is performed. You'll return to the surgical oncologist for the removal. I've already talked to him and set up an appointment for you. As soon as you meet with him, they'll schedule your surgery."

Selena's face felt numb. "Won't the anesthesia harm the baby?"

"I'll be working closely with Dr. Brooks, Selena, so you and the baby will get the best care." Dr. Sanderlin turned to lay the file on her desk. "The first step in finding out how we need to treat this malignancy is to remove it and see how far it's spread. We don't want to wait to remove the tumor and any affected tissue."

Oliver's expression was wooden with control. The only thing that moved was his throat as he swallowed.

"Once we get the results from your surgery, I'll refer you to a medical oncologist. Dr. Dixon has a wonderful reputation and is a very caring doctor. I think you'll like him.

"Though pregnancy makes it more difficult to treat cancer," the doctor continued, "we can treat it. But we won't be able to start you on hormone therapy or radiation until the baby is born. And we can't start chemotherapy until you're at least four months along. We can't treat your cancer as aggressively as we would if you weren't pregnant, but we can fight it and keep it in check until the birth, and then get more aggressive afterward if we need to."

Her throat ached from the effort not to cry. "What about the chemotherapy?"

"Dr. Dixon will go over the protocols with you, but there are drugs we can use which won't impact the baby. He'll give you medications to control your pain and nausea, but your body will be going through a lot."

"And if she weren't pregnant?" Oliver spoke for the first time.

Selena jerked around to look at him while her heart sank. He couldn't be serious.

"If she weren't pregnant, you could attack this thing full-on, right? Wipe it out." There was an edge to Oliver's voice she had never heard before, a blend of rage and pain that gripped her by the throat and brought tears to her eyes.

Dr. Sanderlin paused a moment to study him. "In years past,

termination of the pregnancy was suggested as part of the proto-col for treatment. But we no longer encourage that first thing. I recommend you wait for the results of Selena's surgery and make a decision then. There will still be time if that's the course the two of you settle on." There was no judgment in her tone, only compassion. "Breast cancer is survivable, Ensign Shaker. Selena will have three doctors in her corner, making sure she gets everything she needs to overcome this."

Dr. Sanderlin stood. "I'm going to take Selena down the hall and do a brief exam. You can stay here while we accomplish that, and I'll send her back here when we're done."

As soon as the door closed behind the two women, Oliver leaned forward in his chair, dropped his face onto his hands, closed his eyes, and took deep, gulping gasps of air to keep from vomiting. He finally succeeded in quelling the nausea somewhat.

Dear God, she had cancer. Selena had cancer. He had prayed, hoped it wasn't cancer. He'd prayed for anything but that. And gotten a pregnancy in return.

He paced the office, feeling caged, smothered by his rampag-ing fears and the rage accompanying them.

Had the changes in her hormones triggered the cancer? Would the baby they'd been trying to conceive kill her? And how would he live with that?

His military training said if something was a threat to life, you took it out. End of discussion.

But the baby would delay her treatment, curtail it. He knew Selena would never agree to ending the pregnancy. He'd seen her reaction. That fierce, protective, instinctive response the news had sparked.

How could he fight her maternal instinct? How could he fight his own conscience long enough to argue for termination?

But if it came down to a choice between her or the baby, Selena had to take priority. She had to agree with that. She was everything—to him, to Lucia.

An exam supposed to take a few minutes stretched on to half an hour. Worry set in and Oliver breathed a sigh and rose when Dr. Sanderlin came into the office.

"I thought I'd take a moment to give you an update, Ensign Shaker. May I call you Oliver?"

"Yes, ma'am."

"Have a seat," she pointed at the chair he'd just vacated.

She settled into the chair closest to him. "From the physical exam and the information Selena shared with me, we've determined she's seven weeks pregnant. She's understandably excited and frightened at the same time."

"Could the pregnancy have triggered the cancer?" he asked.

"I don't believe so. From the size and position of the tumor, I'd say it already had a start before she became pregnant."

"She does self-exams every month."

"And that probably helped her detect the tumor before it spread any further but a woman can have a malignancy before it's ever detected, even with a mammogram. When Selena has her surgery, we'll know more about whether it has spread to the lymph nodes. Please try to stay calm, for your benefit as well as hers. Once the tumor has been removed, we'll know where we need to go from there."

He nodded. Her calm settled his roiling gut, but not the fear. He had to get a grip on that himself. "Thanks, Doc."

"Her appointment is on Friday for a preop workup and more tests. We're not dragging our feet on this, Oliver.

He nodded, unable to speak around the knot in his throat.

"I'll be talking to you soon," she said as she stood.

"Okay."

They had never had a quiet marriage. Whether they were making love, fighting, even cooking together, they made plenty of noise. But for the last three days silence had been their language.

And now in the car it resonated between them as loud as a scream.

It took twenty-five minutes to reach home, every second taut with unspoken recriminations. It was almost a relief when she finally asked, "Did you mean it?"

He didn't need her to clarify what she was asking about. "Yeah. I meant it. If it comes down to a choice, I choose you, Selena."

"They're going to take the cancer out and that will be the end of it."

God, he hoped so, prayed it would be so.

"We made this baby just like we did Lucia. It was made with love, Oliver."

He gritted his teeth against a flood of painful emotions. He could turn the tables on her and lay on some guilt, but he wasn't there yet. He'd save that for when it counted. "You said you'd wait and see what they discover during surgery. If it's aggressive, *cara*—" he couldn't say the words.

"This is my body, Oliver. I don't say anything to you when you put yours at risk every time you deploy."

"This is different, Selena."

"No it's not. You put yourself in harm's way to protect those who can't protect themselves. Where is the difference?"

The difference was she was the one who was in danger now. It was only supposed to be him. "I'm a trained soldier. I do everything I can to make sure I come home to you, Selena."

"But there's never any guarantee. I've watched you go to war twice, waited for you to return. I knew there'd be a chance I'd lose you each time. Even when you go somewhere to train, with all the dangerous stuff you do, I know there's always a possibility you could be injured or killed in an accident. That's my reality." She laid her hand on his thigh and his muscles tightened. "This is our family, Oliver. I need you to be as supportive of me as I am of you."

He'd never heard her talk like this before. And whatever he'd planned to say couldn't stand up to everything she'd just dumped on him. So he said nothing at all.

CHAPTER FIVE

S ELENA PICKED UP the loan application she'd been assessing and scanned the applicant information again. With every word her stomach pitched a little further off-kilter. She dropped the paper and closed her eyes, willing the morning sickness, which had finally kicked in today, to ease.

Two seconds later she lost the battle and darted down the hall to the ladies' room. She'd barely made it into one of the stalls when she lost the breakfast of yogurt and granola she'd eaten an hour before. For ten minutes she heaved until she thought her lungs might come up and her stomach muscles ached. Despite the ick factor, though the floor looked clean, she sat on the tile for another five minutes and simply breathed in and out, resting against the stall door.

She was having a baby. Somehow morning sickness made it more real than even the positive pregnancy test and hearing the doctor say it.

A pair of low-heeled black pumps appeared at one side of the stall. "I've made you a cup of hot tea and scared up some soda crackers." It was Sheila Masters, the secretary she shared with two other loan officers at the bank.

"You are an angel, Sheila. Thank you."

"Do you need me to call someone to pick you up?"

"No. Going home won't help. This isn't a virus."

Sheila remained silent for a moment. "Does it mean what I think it means?"

She hadn't told her family. Or even her closest friends. She was allowing this cancer thing to drain every bit of joy from her life. Was she keeping the baby a secret because of the door Oliver had opened...even though she'd insisted it remain closed? She cupped her hand around her lower abdomen. *Hell, no!*

"Yes, I'm having a baby." The strong sound of her own voice helped her feel more positive, more certain. *The baby Oliver and I wanted.*

"Congratulations!"

"Thank you. I haven't told Mr. Watts yet, so I'd appreciate it if you'd keep it quiet until I have a chance to speak with him today."

"As the English say, mum's the word."

She smiled at the joke. "Thanks."

She'd have to tell her boss everything and let him know she'd also be out several weeks after the surgery. Would they hold her job for her if she had to be out for an extended time? Without her salary, their financial situation would take a big hit. How would they make it?

She realized she was falling back into the pit of worry again and shoved it away. They'd figure it out some way.

She staggered to her feet and leaned against the stall door for a moment, till she was certain her stomach had settled. A cup of tea did sound good. She entered her office to find it sitting in the center of her blotter with the crackers. Once again she breathed a relieved sigh and mentally thanked Sheila for being female and understanding.

She returned to processing the loan application, then called her boss's extension to ask for a few minutes of his time.

Because of her pregnancy, more blood tests and several more ultrasounds had been done of her breasts and armpits. With every test she became more certain the outcome of the surgery might not be what they'd hoped.

She kept her thoughts and feelings to herself, for fear of upsetting Oliver even more. This was up to her to deal with. It was her body. Her life. As much as she loved him, he lived on the periphery of her and Lucia's lives much of the time. He seemed content with the arrangement. He loved them, she was certain of that. But, like most men, he identified so completely with what he did, he was a Special Forces operator first and a husband and father second. She'd accepted the reality long ago.

But things were different now. She didn't have time to pander to his ego.

Her surgery was scheduled for next Friday. Two weeks from her first visit to the ObGyn. The baby would be nine weeks along and would be about the size of a grape. She was going to count her own progress through the weeks of her pregnancy. She was going to concentrate on having a healthy baby and doing whatever she had to do to stay alive.

Clinging to her resolve, she went down the hall to speak to her boss.

THE DESERT SUN beat against the back of Oliver's neck, despite his Boonie hat. He should have tied a bandana around his neck before he'd taken the controls. Why the fuck was it so much hotter out here? It was the same state, the same sun.

Intellectually he knew all the reasons, but this one small irritation fed the black mood which had festered ever since he and Selena had left the doctor's office. He was angry because it was easier to feel rage than to acknowledge the fear. Rage at God for letting this happen, rage at Selena for being sick, for choosing a fetus over their family, rage at himself for not being home enough, not spending enough time with her, not doing all the things a husband should do.

Coming out to Camp Billy Machen for this updated training was a blessing. He was no good to Selena in his current frame of mind, and when he'd told her he needed to go, she seemed relieved. Or was it because she was resolved his job should come first even now? God, he didn't know how to feel anymore.

Oliver gripped the black control box to the drone like he'd just been thrown a lifeline. It gave him an excuse to concentrate on something else. The electronic screen flashed as he moved the toggle, directing the surveillance drone to fly at a specific speed and altitude.

It was like flying a souped-up model airplane using a flight simulator. The engine was designed to be quieter, and the powerful camera attached to its small fuselage homed in on objects, mapped their location, and could use infrared technology to detect heat signatures. It also sent recorded images to the computer Hawk had balanced on the hood of their Humvee. The drone was an expensive device designed to surveil the enemy and save lives.

Six of his teammates, three two-man teams in Desert Patrol Vehicles, DPVs, were out there waiting to be located Though the DPVs were no longer used as much as they had been during Desert Storm, they still came in handy for training and at times were fun to drive over the rough terrain.

The only down side was they had no air conditioning, and after four hours out in the sun, the guys would be eager to return to base and get out of the heat. But they had to be detected before they could do so. Oliver switched the camera to infrared, swooped the drone down to two hundred feet, and skimmed across the area.

The topographic landscape flying past the drone's lens looked similar to what they'd experienced in Afghanistan and Iraq. For a moment he flashed back to the dry, sandy heat. The smell of the place would be forever locked in his memory. It reeked of poverty, suffering, death and war.

He designed his flight path to cover the grid he'd been assigned. Two red heat signatures, moving west, popped up on the screen and he swooped overhead and took a picture of the armored dune buggy decked out with a gun mount on the reinforced framework. Hawk, his team leader, leaned his six foot four frame back against the front quarter panel of their Humvee and watched the screen from over Oliver's shoulder. Hawk radioed the two men detected in the vehicle that they'd been spotted and to return to base.

Two more DPVs to go and they'd get out of the heat for a while. Three minutes later the drone caught up to the next vehicle moving south and tagged them with a picture. Five long minutes followed until he discovered the next two men, who were parked and working on one of the wheels on their vehicle. Oliver switched off the infrared to identify them.

"Bowie and Doc are having a mechanical issue," he said as he took the picture.

Hawk nodded. "We'll swing by their location on our way back to base and see if we can assist or give them a ride."

"I have their location saved so we can track them with GPS."

"Sounds like a plan."

Oliver pushed the drone to a higher altitude and directed it back to them. He circled to get the lay of the land, and finding a bare strip where traffic from Humvees, trucks, DPVs and the occasional motorcycle had cleared a path, and lined up for a landing. The drone swooped down and he slowed its speed. The wheels extended and the machine settled on the hard-packed, bumpy sand twenty feet or so from their ride.

"Have you thought about taking flying lessons, Greenback?" Hawk asked as they loaded the drone into the back of the vehicle. "Looks like you've already got the landing part down."

"Private lessons are too expensive, but if you can sweet-talk command into paying, I'm definitely up for it."

"I'll see what I can do."

He felt a brief moment of excitement before reality hit. He couldn't volunteer for extra duty or training while Selena was sick. What was he thinking? This goddamn waiting was holding their lives up. He needed to tell Hawk what was going on, but, Jesus, his team leader's mother had died of breast cancer while he was down range. It was hard as hell to bring it up.

He needed to come up with something else to talk about until he figured out what he wanted to say to Hawk.

"Will Brett make it back for the wedding?" he asked.

Hawk frowned. "You've asked the six-million-dollar question. I hope so. Tess is going to be one very disappointed bride if he doesn't."

"Maybe she can cancel at the last minute and have it on the beach or in someone's back yard when he makes it."

"There are a hundred and fifty guests coming. A quarter of them military."

Or maybe not. "I told Selena they could Skype the ceremony, and then have another when Brett hits CONUS."

Hawk glanced in his direction. "If it comes down to the wire, it wouldn't be a bad idea as last-minute saves go. I'll put it out there."

"It was insane to attempt a big, fancy wedding. If Selena and I hadn't already done the deed before I went into the teams, we'd have eloped or had a simple ceremony with our closest friends, like you and Zoe."

"In our case it was good and bad at the same time, Greenback. Good we got hitched, but somewhere down the road, Zoe may regret not having the big show. But there are worse things. I missed her whole pregnancy."

"At least you were there for the birth. I missed it all." He couldn't avoid this pregnancy or Selena's illness. What would he have done if he were out of the states when she'd gotten ill? His breathing hitched.

His own struggles brought Derrick Armstrong to mind. "Any news about Strong Man?"

Hawk remained silent for a moment. "He took a plea. Four years' prison in a military facility and a dishonorable discharge. He avoided facing us, but it also saved the team some unwanted publicity in the SEAL community and the public."

Silence stretched for several beats.

"It was a waste," Oliver mussed.

"Yeah."

"Why would he try and kill his best friend?"

"It had to be him. Doc and Bowie were together during the op. Flash was on the roof across the street. We all saw him exit the structure after the explosion, and besides, he was busy taking out insurgents up there. The others saw the muzzle flashes and the guys above them going down."

"Who did Doc see going back in besides you?"

"Maybe Derrick had a change of heart. But I don't know how he got back out before the place blew. And I sure as shit didn't see him inside."

That last mission with Brett had changed the whole makeup of the team. They'd lost Brett and Flash, first to other challenges, then to other teams, and Derrick Armstrong to prison. What had happened would remain a mystery until Brett remembered what happened or Derrick decided to man up and come clean.

Five minutes later they pulled up beside Bowie and Doc. "We've broken an axel." Bowe announced. "I've called in our coordinates and requested a tow."

Hawk got out of the Humvee. "If the motor pool has the co-ordinates, they can come out and get the buggy. You can ride in with us."

"Roger that!" Doc's redhead complexion was flushed from the heat and sun, and his freckles looked darker in the strong light. He jogged around the car to get in on the other side.

"Guess he's ready to go back to base," Bowie said, his dark eyebrows quirked. He jerked the door open and climbed in.

Teammates and friends since BUD/S, the two guys could read each other's body language in the dark and instinctively knew what the other was thinking. Oliver had seen the communication between them at work. Oliver wondered why he hadn't bonded with one of the other guys like that.

Maybe because most of them had been single and he was married. After BUD/S, there'd always been beer runs and parties the single guys had organized in between trainings, but he'd gone home to Selena. He'd been a married man of three years before taking on the teams.

He sure as shit could use a friend to confide in right now. His gaze swung to Hawk. He'd been through the breast cancer thing with his mother. He'd understand his need to be with Selena as much as possible.

Hawk's wife Zoe had scars from a hit and run accident and had physical issues from it. He didn't seem to give a damn about her limp or her scars. He was crazy about her. Every guy in the team knew it.

Hawk would identify with what he was going through. He had to tell him, and he was going to need some time off for Selena's surgery and other treatments. Fill out the paperwork.

Anxiety shot heat into his face, nullifying the cold air blowing out of the vents. And his breathing quickened.

Hawk pulled away from the DPV and drove east.

"Stop looking at your cell phone," Bowie said in tune to the click of their seat belts. "You're acting like a girl."

"Shut the fuck up." Oliver caught Doc's movement from the corner of his eye as he flipped a half-hearted backhanded punch to Bowie's solar plexus and Bowie umphed in pain. "You're just pissed because you're between girls right now."

The car seemed to close in around Oliver, growing smaller and smaller, the seat belt too tight over his chest. He tugged at it to relieve the pressure.

"Dude, I'm always between girls." Oliver knew he was smiling from the tone of his voice. "Remember those twins? And they were identical in every way."

As the sound of his own breathing got harsher, his heartbeat louder, pumping through his ears, Bowie and Doc's voices grew muffled.

"Yeah, I remember them. How could I forget? You've been rehashing the details for the past year. Makes me think you're spoiled to multiples and can't man up to a single woman anymore."

The sweat coating Oliver's skin turned to ice water and nausea rolled over him.

"Doc you're not getting the whole picture man. We're talking hands, mouths, tits—"

"Stop!" The word exploded from Oliver. Hawk slammed on the brakes.

The seat belt locked and jerked Oliver back before he hit the dash. He slammed open the door, and the inferno of heat outside rushed in with the dust stirred by their tires. He fought free of the seat belt, rolled out of the car, and barely caught himself before doing a face-plant in the dirt.

He choked on the dust, and his attempts to draw breath turned to hacking coughs interspersed with sobs while tears streamed down his face, as much from his efforts to breathe as from emotion.

"Where's the med kit, Hawk?" Doc's voice came from within the vehicle as the other doors flew open.

"In back with the drone."

Hawk and Bowie grabbed him under each arm and dragged him free of the dust cloud and into the meager shade of a Joshua tree.

Doc squatted in front of him and took his pulse. While he coughed up the grit he'd breathed and swallowed, Oliver focused on his broad Irish face. It took some time to beat back the emotion still clawing at his chest, keeping his breathing tight. He rubbed his shirtsleeve over his eyes and face to wipe away his tears. They'd think it was from the dust, wouldn't they?

"Just take a few more deep breaths, Greenback. Are you having pressure in your chest? Any pain?"

Any pain? He dropped his head back and shook it. "I thought I was going to hurl. It must have been the heat." SEALs weren't supposed to have anxiety attacks. He was supposed to be in control. Keep his emotions in hand. He braced a forearm on his updrawn knee and rested his forehead upon it.

Doc rested a hand on his shoulder.

He'd just lied to a friend to protect his ego. He wasn't in control. He wasn't in control of anything. They were going to cut into his wife and take her breast. Maybe both of them. Time to man up. "It isn't the heat, guys." He blinked his eyes furiously when the tears threatened again. "Selena's pregnant and she's got breast cancer. They're going to do a mastectomy next week."

Doc's eyes widened with shock. Hawk and Bowie froze with

the same motionlessness they used when terrorists tiptoed close to their location.

Hawk was the first to move, and dropped to one knee next to him. "What the fuck are you doing here? You should be with her."

"She's working, taking care of as much bank business as she can before she has the surgery. We have to stay busy and fill every moment...otherwise we'd both go crazy." He raked his fingers through his hair and squeezed his temples. "I have to get my head straight before I can be any use to her, Hawk. I haven't slept since I found out. I'm just so fucked up right now."

Hawk's face showed all the pain he was feeling. "I didn't get an opportunity to be there for Mom when she was going through this. She didn't tell me she was sick until it was too late. You have an opportunity to be Selena's wingman through all this, Green-back. You need to get your shit together and step up. I'm calling Zoe and Trish. They'll get the ball rolling on that end. She'll need backup while you're out here." Hawk jerked his cell phone out and ran his thumb over the face to open it.

"She hasn't even called her mom and sisters, Hawk. We won't know how bad it is until after the surgery." Oliver scrubbed his face with his hands. Hawk was right. He was making this all about his needs and ignoring hers. He'd been such a shit to her before leaving home for this training—angry, distant, and silent. Like he'd been for days. He was blaming her for being sick when there wasn't a damn thing she could do about it. He'd really fucked up.

"L.T., I'd like to be the one to talk to them."

Hawk handed him the phone.

SELENA DUMPED THE shopping bags and her purse next to the front door and turned to check on Lucia's progress up the front walk. The backpack her daughter wore was almost as big as she was, but she insisted on carrying it back and forth to daycare with her favorite toy for naptime. Thank goodness this last round of antibiotics seemed to have done the trick, and the troublesome ear infection was gone.

She was holding open the door for Lucia when Zoe Yazzie's car pulled into the drive. The doors opened and five women got out—Zoe, Hawk's wife, and her soon to be sister-in-law, Tess Kelly. Trish Marks, the unofficial leader of the wives' group and wife of Langley Marks, Hawk's XO. Marsha Jackson, Oliver's commanding officer's wife, and then Zoe's mom, Clara Weaver, brought up the rear.

She studied each of their expressions while they walked toward her. Had something happened to Oliver? Anxiety hit her like a thunderbolt and her heart rate shot up.

"Oliver called us," Zoe said, setting her fears to rest. "He and the guys will be out there a couple more days, and he thought a little backup for you might not be a bad idea. Just in case."

Selena heaved a sigh. Just what had he told them?

Zoe grasped Lucia's hand, "Hello, Miss Lucia. How was school today?" She walked with Lucia up the two steps and Selena stood back to let them in.

"Nap time sucks," Lucia declared, her words so clear all the women laughed.

"She learned the expression from one of the older children and loves saying it," Selena giggled.

Everyone filed in, but no one sat down. Marsha Jackson stepped forward. "Oliver called us all and told us everything. His exact words were, 'I've already been an asshole, and she's already pissed at me, so it won't matter if she gets mad at me for telling you.'" Marsha swallowed. "We're a family, Selena. We all want to stand with you through whatever comes. We're here to schedule help times for while you recover from surgery. You'll need it, and we want to do at least that much."

The tight ball of hurt and confusion left by Oliver's defection to Camp Billy Machen eased and, though Selena attempted to stem the tears, her eyes still filled. She brushed them aside and offered them all a smile. "I'm not mad at him for telling you. I've wanted to but—it was just too much."

"We understand," Trish said, hugging her.

"Come on into the kitchen and we'll have some iced tea and talk."

When they were settled at the kitchen table Selena looked at each expectant face, opened herself to experience their genuine, heartfelt desire to support her, and spilled it all. After they all cried a little, they got busy making a list of things she might need help with following surgery.

"I want Oliver to save as many of his emergency leave days as possible in case we need them."

"I'm retired and Russell is still working, so I'm available during the day," Clara said as she lifted Lucia up in her lap and handed her a slice of cheese and some crackers from the plate Selena had put out.

They wrote down their schedules, then worked out a rotation for each day.

"Oliver will be here at night as long as they don't have another training."

"He'll want to take off a few days to be with you, Selena," Zoe said.

Would he? After his first rush of support he'd been so distant. Especially since the doctor's appointment and everything she'd said in the car.

"I'm trying to stay positive. Excuse me for a second, please." She stood and went back to retrieve something from the bags she'd dropped by the door that she wanted to share.

She'd designed the baby announcements at work during her lunch break. She'd dropped them by a one-hour copy place on her way to get Lucia from daycare and picked them up on her way home. The women laughed when she saw the grape-shaped cartoon, and immediately set to helping her address the envelopes.

"Is the baby really the size of a grape?" Tess asked, holding up the announcement. Her auburn hair shone with copper highlights and, though she was the closest to her age, Selena felt centuries older.

"It will be by next week," Selena said. "It's about the size of a sesame seed right now."

Tess shook her head. "Amazing. If the baby's a girl you could name her Chablis," Tess said with a grin.

"Oh, my God, that sounds like a stripper," Trish said.

"Or Champagne…no, wait, it would be a stripper's name, too," Zoe chimed in.

"What about Barbera or Margaux? Those are wine terms, but don't sound so stripperesque," Tess suggested.

"Is stripperesque even a word?" Marsha asked as she sealed an envelope.

"And how do you even know Barbera and Margaux are wine terms?" Zoe demanded.

"California is wine country. I had to write a story about one of the vineyards."

"If we're going to name her after a wine, it will have to be an Italian wine," Selena said firmly, desperate to keep the laughter and the feeling of normalcy going.

"Chianti," Clara suggested. When they all looked at her, she shrugged. "It's the only Italian wine I know."

"Rosato, it's a rose-colored Italian wine. Her name could be Rosa," Tess suggested.

"Actually Rosa might work. My mother's name is Rosalie but my father often calls her Rosa."

"That's so sweet."

It was. Just the simple pastime of discussing baby names gave her something to hold onto and made her feel as though her life could go on despite the cancer.

She had to hold onto the life inside her. It was the most important positive thing in her life right now. If only she could get Oliver to see it for the blessing it was, instead of a stumbling block to survival which he believed it to be. Once they took the cancer out and she was well again, he'd see things differently.

CHAPTER SIX

"WE HAD TO take a little more breast tissue than I had hoped, Selena." The surgical oncologist was tall and thin, with exaggerated features which seemed crammed into the center of his face. He projected confidence and a positive attitude.

But Oliver's heart sank. They had been talking lumpectomy, then a modified mastectomy, and now they were talking more. It had been thirty-six hours since the surgery and, aside from being in some moderate pain, Selena seemed to be soldiering up, but he'd seen how her fingers had traced over the area and been worried when he watched her face as she did it.

"I wanted to go back over some of the information I've shared with you before. We had to take the nipple, but we've left you plenty of skin to use for reconstruction later. The border of the tumor was wider than we had at first expected. The important thing is we were able to remove all the diseased tissue. And there was no muscular involvement."

Her features were pale, but she didn't seem surprised.

"We will have the pathology on the seven lymph nodes we removed by next week. I'll discuss follow-up treatment once we have pathology results, so I'll need to see you a week from today. The nurse will set up the appointment for you. I'll want to check the site and make sure it is healing as expected, and we'll also remove your temporary drains. The nurse will show you how to empty them in the meantime. You don't need to change the dressing. I'll do it during your appointment in a few days. Just keep the site dry, relax, and allow yourself to heal. If you see any unusual swelling, or have severe pain, don't hesitate to contact my office or come in to the ER."

Once the doctor left, Oliver sat on the edge of the bed and cradled her hand.

"Did you know it had spread more than they'd first thought?" he asked.

"I suspected it had. They did so many ultrasound images, especially in the area under my arm." Dark shadows were stamped beneath her eyes. With so many nurses and techs going in and out of the surgical rooms, sleep, when it came, was brief. "My breast is gone, Oliver."

"I know."

Her gaze held an uncertainty. "You've always loved my breasts."

"I've always loved the rest of you, too, *cara mia.*"

He knew he'd said the right thing when she leaned in to rest against him. Careful of the tubes, he slipped an arm around her and stroked her hair. "It's going to be okay." What else could he say?

THE PAIN WAS nothing compared to the hollow feeling she got every time she saw the spot where her breast had been. Even with the bandages pulled tight around her, she could see the concave shape of her loss.

She'd read somewhere the surgery severed the nerves so she would no longer experience sensation in that breast anymore. And what if the cancer spread to the other one? If only she could be numb all over right now.

She needed to be home and away from this place where they had disfigured her. She'd had no idea how she'd feel afterward. She'd been concentrating on just getting past the surgery. Nothing else. But now she felt so much pain and anger.

"What matters is, the cancer is gone, *carina*," Oliver said, his voice soft.

But it might not be gone. She couldn't take radiation therapy to be certain. What more would they do?

Exhaustion rushed up to envelop her, and she settled against Oliver's shoulder and closed her eyes. He loved her. But men were usually squeamish about these things. Would his reaction be different because of his experiences?

And they still couldn't seem to talk about the baby. How long would their silence last?

BACKUP WAITED FOR them at home. Oliver hoped he'd done the right thing. Selena needed to know how much she was loved. And maybe it would make up for some of the shit they were both dealing with right now.

Because the medical staff couldn't use the typical diagnostic tests due to her pregnancy, they were still in the dark about the spread of the disease. No radioactive dye to check the lymph nodes. No radiation until she'd delivered the baby. No hormone therapy to starve the cancer and make sure it didn't come back. Pregnancy tied their hands in so many ways.

The hurt look so clear in Selena's eyes gripped him by the throat every time. A part of her was gone now, and she was grieving… he was, too. But she was alive. Which was all that mattered.

They reached home to find Hawk sitting on the small stoop.

"What's Hawk doing here, Oliver?" Her hand lingered against her blouse, covering the spot where her breast had been.

"I asked him to run an errand for me."

While Oliver went around to help her out, Hawk came over to greet them, but his gaze remained on Selena's face.

Though she was dressed as normal in jeans and a button-up blouse, she moved as though every step was over broken glass.

"Zoe said to call if you need anything at all. Goes for me, too."

She nodded and made an effort to smile. "Thank you, Hawk."

He nodded and turned to Oliver. "The package is inside, Greenback. I'm shoving off so you two can rest."

"Thanks, Hawk."

"What package, Oliver?"

"Just something I thought you might need." He helped her up the stoop.

"I remember how you did this when I came home from the hospital with Lucia," she said, her voice soft.

Her dark eyes, so expressive, lifted to his face.

He wasn't ready for this conversation. "In the teams we plan each step we take with care, but at the end of the day, when we've done all we can, all we think of is home. We've done all we can for the moment, and now it's time to think of home."

He opened the door and shoved it wide. Selena's mother rose from the couch. She appeared to be as nervous as Oliver felt. As she took a step toward the door, her features, so similar to Selena's, crumpled with emotion. When Selena walked toward her and buried her face against her mother's shoulder, Oliver knew he'd done the right thing. He closed the door to give them a few minutes while he went back out to retrieve Selena's small over-night bag.

He was finally starting to get it. As a SEAL he stood alone as a man, but together as a member of his team. And at home Selena did the same, but the other half of her team was usually gone, leaving her stranded. It was hard to reach out to family and friends who lived outside the life and explain the psychology. She carried just as much on her shoulders, and she was used to doing it alone. Then when it came time to ask for help, it made it harder for her to say the words or even admit she needed it. He'd need to be her backup and tell people what she couldn't say herself.

When he re-entered the house, Rosalie, Selena's mother, still held her, but they'd gravitated to the couch.

He dumped the overnight bag in the bedroom and went into

the kitchen to fix them all something to drink. Though it was just past noon, he craved a beer, or something stronger, but chose a glass of iced tea instead.

He slid the glasses on coasters in front of them.

Selena's eyes, wet with tears, settled on him. "Thank you, Oliver."

HE SPENT THE day catching up on yard work and fixing a small leak in the storage building roof while Selena slept and was babied by her mother, which was exactly what she needed.

At five o'clock he picked Lucia up from daycare. She'd be excited to have Selena home, for, as much as she'd enjoyed having Daddy's undivided attention for an evening or two, she'd gotten teary at bedtime each night when Momma wasn't there. She'd never been separated from Selena for more than a few hours. He'd lain with her in her tiny twin bed until she finally fell asleep, and then lay awake in their bed, staring at the ceiling and alert for the phone in case the hospital called. It was easier to take power naps in the chair at the hospital than to sleep without Selena beside him.

"Mommy's home and she's excited to see you," he said as he helped Lucia get her backpack off and settled her in her booster seat in the back of the van.

"Mommy's home!" A smile lit her entire face. "I'm e-sighted too."

Oliver smiled at the mispronounced word but didn't correct her.

"Mommy has a sore spot on her chest right here." He pointed to his right pectoral muscle. "We have to be careful not to touch it until it's well."

Lucia's eyes widened. "I won't touch it," she said in a whisper.

"She's missed you very much."

"I missed Mommy, too."

He fastened the seat belt and gave her a kiss.

"Grandma Rose is at the house, too. She's come to visit us."

Lucia grinned. "Grandma Rose?"

"Yes, she came to see you and to help Mommy until she feels better."

"We Skype Grandma Rose."

What did it say when your three year old knew how to Skype? "Yes, I know you do. You'll see her in person as soon as we're home. What do you want to listen to on the radio?"

"*Twinkle, Twinkle.*"

Half wishing he hadn't asked, he put in the CD of nursery songs as soon as he was belted in and cranked the ignition.

He listened to Lucia sing along with the CD. She knew almost every word to the songs. Who cared if, during *Whole World In His Hands*, it was Ho Wood?

For the first time he allowed himself to wonder if the baby Selena was carrying would be as smart. If it survived. If Selena could carry it to term. *If-if-if.* How was he supposed to feel? How could he promise to lay his life down to protect other people's children and not do the same for his own? But it wasn't his life hanging in the balance, it was his wife's. The guilt and pain of this struggle were constant.

He turned the thoughts off. He couldn't think about it. He had to concentrate on Selena. He was more worried about her emotional state right now. Those few moments of grief at the hospital would not be the last.

Though they'd traveled to New York several times since Lucia was born, and both their families had come to visit when they could, Grandma Rose was someone new in Lucia's world. She was both excited and a little shy for all of five minutes, then gave Rosalie enthusiastic hugs and kisses. She sat on the couch between Selena and her mother and jabbered away, filling them both in on everything she had done at daycare. Her vocabulary was growing through the lessons she was taught at daycare and through music. But her pronunciation was sometimes comical.

For the rest of the evening, Grandma Rose held center stage and did most of the cooking. At eight o'clock Selena ran out of steam and went to bed, and he got Lucia tucked in soon after.

It was as he was checking on Selena for the fourth time and easing the bedroom door shut, Rosalie caught him in a hug. "She's going to be okay. She's strong, and she has you in her corner."

"I know," he said trying to be positive, though the fear was still there.

"You don't have to entertain me if you want to go on to bed. I know you've been running between home and the hospital. I have my e-reader and the television. If Lucia wakes up, I'll take care of her."

He didn't want to go to bed, but he did want to lie beside his wife and just know she was there.

"Frank and I have had a long marriage. And it's because we've leaned on each other we've made it when other friends didn't. You and Selena have that kind of marriage."

"I haven't been home nearly enough."

"But when you are, you pour everything you have into it, Oliver. She knows you love her."

He nodded, though the guilt wouldn't go away. He knew the other married men experienced it too. More marriages ended than survived the teams. "I put fresh linens on the guest room bed and laid towels out for you. Help yourself to anything you need."

Rosalie patted his arm and murmured goodnight. She went back into the living room.

He slipped into the bedroom, took a quick shower, and eased in beside Selena.

Her eyes opened and she studied his face for a moment. "I'm very proud of what you do, Oliver. You have nothing to feel guilty about. I went into our marriage with my eyes wide open."

So she had heard what they'd said. "You didn't count on the teams."

"No, but it was something you needed to do and I understood. I still do."

Just as she needed to carry their baby. He flinched away from the thought. "You've read the code we follow."

"Yes."

"I take it very seriously, Selena."

"I know you do."

"I was thinking you need your own code."

She sifted her fingers through the curls on his forehead, and he sighed, and then lifted her palm to his lips. "Repeat after me. I will *never* give up."

She looked into his eyes for a long moment, and a lone tear streaked across her nose and onto the pillow. "I will *never* give up."

"If adversity knocks me down, I *will* pick myself up."

"If adversity knocks me down. I *will* pick myself up."

"I will use every ounce of my strength to fight."

Her voice cracked but she said the words. "I will use every ounce of my strength to fight."

"I will never stop fighting."

"I will never stop fighting."

He wiped her tears away with the sheet. "I love you. No matter what happens, I'll love you."

She nodded. He wanted to wrap her in his arms and cuddle her, but the tubes were there, and he was afraid he might accidentally hurt her. Instead he laced his fingers through hers and held tight.

CHAPTER SEVEN

S ELENA STARED AT the huge clump of hair in the drain. There was more and more each day. So much she'd bought a screen for the tub so it wouldn't go down the drain and clog.

This latest loss looked like a small animal had drowned in the shower. She braced herself before turning to face the mirror over the sink. Her heart fell and tears glazed her eyes. She'd thought seeing the flat, nipple-less area where her breast had been removed would be the worst shock she'd sustain, but seeing her hair fall out had a suck factor all its own.

They had been so upbeat about her prognosis until the three lymph nodes had come back positive. Three lymph nodes had made the difference between chemo and no chemo.

And this latest suggestion by her medical oncologist had hit her hardest. He wanted her to have her ovaries removed once the baby was delivered.

She stared at her reflection. She didn't want Oliver to see her like this. Ragged. Unkempt. She stared at her reflection. Would she lose her eyebrows and lashes too? With her Italian features, she'd look like a modern day Mona Lisa. She tried an enigmatic smile. It ended up more a grimace.

She lowered the lid onto the toilet, sat down and gave free vent to the tears for the next five minutes. Only five minutes, because it was all the time she could spare to dwell on this loss.

With difficulty, she dragged her composure back into place, mopped her face, and blew her nose. Rifling through a lavatory drawer, she found a pair of scissors, but just did a few halfhearted snips before putting them down. Why do a job when an expert was available?

She picked up her cell phone and dialed Trish and Langley's number.

Langley answered the phone with a brusque, "Hello."

"Langley, this is Selena."

"Hey, pretty lady. You okay?"

"Yes, I just called to ask a favor."

"Shoot."

She explained what she needed. "If I swing by, could you do it before I have to go to work?"

"Yeah, I can do it."

"I can be there in about twenty minutes."

"I'll be here."

She dressed, took her nausea medication, and applied a light makeup to cover the bruise-like shadows beneath her eyes, then wrapped a scarf around her head.

Langley opened the door to her and ushered her into the kitchen. "You lucked out, the clan just left for school with Trish."

"Oliver took Lucia to daycare for me."

Langley put a chair in the middle of the kitchen floor and whipped out a barber's cape from his kit, and then produced scissors, clippers, and a comb.

Suddenly shy, Selena studied his lantern-jawed, homely, handsome face. "It looks pretty bad."

"It'll be okay, honey," he said, his gaze steady.

Her throat tight, she sat in the chair and dropped her bag on the floor next to her. The vulnerability of having such a widely recognized cancer side-effect out where everyone could see was as painful as her aching joints. Everywhere she went people stared.

Langley unwrapped the scarf and laid it on the counter. He ran his fingers over the long strands still hanging in there at the back. Her hair was so thin on top she could see her scalp. She knew what his fingers came away with when he drew a deep breath. "I'll need to use scissors first, take some length off so the clippers won't pull."

Selena swallowed. "Okay."

He got out the scissors. With every fallen strand her head felt lighter, and she decided to equate each one with shedding yet another worry. She relaxed and gazed absently at the small ray of sunshine reflecting off the toaster. This was just one more thing she had to endure to stay well until the baby was born. At the flutter of the baby's kick, she rested a hand against the side of her distended abdomen, enjoying the moment of communion with her unborn child.

Langley turned on the clippers, and, starting at her hairline in front, then going from front to back in long, slow, smooth strips. The fuzz scattered across the barber's cape looked like black feathers. When he turned the clippers off, she twisted around to look up at him.

He cupped her naked head with his large hand, and his Adam's apple bobbed as he swallowed. "All done."

"Thank you, Langley."

"Welcome." He tugged the Velcro catch on the barber's cape free, shook it off, and turned away to fold it and stuff it in the case with the clippers.

"I can help you clean up."

"I got it covered. You better scoot or you'll be late."

"Does it—It looks better this way, doesn't it?"

Langley turned to face her. His smile looked natural and eased the tightness in her chest. "Prettiest G.I. haircut I've ever seen."

Selena smiled. But as soon as her fingers explored the area behind her ear, tears threatened. She dropped her hand, jerked her chin up, and squared her shoulders. "Bald is beautiful."

Langley laughed. "You've convinced me."

Selena shot him her best smile, scooped up her purse, and rose from the chair. "I owe you some double chocolate brownies." She gave him a quick hug.

"With nuts," he added, giving her a gentle squeeze in return.

"With nuts."

She murmured, "Bald is beautiful," all the way to work.

LANGLEY'S CALL WAS only a small surprise.

Oliver rubbed a hand over his jaw and jerked the wheel to avoid a slow-moving delivery van as it turned in front of him. "How was she when she left?"

"She was holding it together. As she was leaving, she said 'bald is beautiful,' and nearly drove me to my knees."

"I understand." He did. With every new thing she had to face—the treatment, the nausea, sore joints, aches and pains—she just kept going. She clung to her job as a small spot of normalcy in her otherwise cancer-fighting-filled life. But how much longer would she be able to work?

"If you have any ideas how I can help her face this, let me know."

"Roger that. I'll give it some thought."

"Thanks, Lang."

"Whatever it takes, my friend. See you at the base."

"I'm on my way."

There were things about her treatment she wasn't sharing with him. He couldn't go to every doctor's appointment, though he'd made it to every chemo treatment thus far. The first had been terrifying. Though he'd tried to remain calm and reassuring, her anxiety about the baby had spread to him. Watching the fluid flow into her vein and wondering if she would have a reaction, or if it would send her into premature labor, had been the worst four hours of his life.

And now, even though Selena covered the evidence with scarves, he'd seen what was happening to her hair in the shower, on the bathroom floor, even in the clothesbasket. And there wasn't a damn thing anyone could do about it.

And the day after chemo, she was always knocked off her feet by nausea and exhaustion. And he was so fucking helpless to protect her from any of it.

He ran his hand over his own tight curls. He'd shave his hair off, too, but she loved running her fingers through it when they lay in bed and talked each night. What could he do to offer her support? He'd ask the other guys.

He turned the car toward Coronado. They would be transported to Miramar, where they were to fly out for a HALO jump, high altitude, low opening. When in CONUS (the Continental U.S.) they were required to do jumps to keep their skills razor sharp.

Doc and Bowie looked up as he exited the car and moved to meet him. With a quick greeting they entered the storage facility to retrieve their jump gear, so they each could spread theirs out on tables for close inspection. He made himself concentrate on double-checking every strap and buckle. Then inspected his face mask, hose, and oxygen supply, even though they'd done the same thing the day before in preparation.

Hawk entered with the three new guys of the unit—Jeff Sizemore, call sign Bullet, their new sniper; Seaman Jack Logan, call sign Box for his COM expertise; and Seaman Kelsey Tyler, call sign Celt, a member of the fire team. Langley Marks followed behind them.

What if something happened to Selena while he was twenty-nine thousand feet in the air and he couldn't get to her right away? What if something were to happen to him while she was going through all this? He loved what he did, knew the members of his team depended on him. But right now she needed him more and, since they weren't deployed into a war zone, they could do without him, or transfer someone in to complete the team until he could return.

He reached for his phone and stepped away from the group to call Selena. The bank's automated system asked him to key in the extension and put him through to her office. Her voice sounded the same as always when she answered. "Selena Shaker speaking. What can I do for you?"

"I just wanted to check on you," he replied.

"I'm fine. Just working on some paperwork and getting ready for a meeting."

"Feeling okay?"

"Just a little tired."

Of course she wouldn't mention the hair thing until he saw her tonight. "I'll be out of touch for a while. If anything happens, you know the backup plan."

They'd devised a list of people to call who would stand in for him until he could reach her. What they hell did that say about his priorities?

"Yes. But I'm sure I won't need to call anyone. I'm having a good day. Even my stomach has decided to cooperate."

A good day after she'd had Langley shave her head? He smiled. His wife was amazing. "Good, I'm glad, *cara*." She'd been plagued with morning sickness the first few months, and now the nausea from the chemo had kicked in to take over. She must sometimes feel like the problems and physical stressors would never end.

He wouldn't stress her out by telling her what training they were involved in today. She'd worry. "Should you have to call, Langley will be coordinating today. He'll have his cell and he'll know how to get me to wherever you need me, as fast as humanly possible."

"Okay. I have a doctor's appointment later. So I'll be fine. Be careful."

"Roger that. Love you."

"Love you, too."

"Everything okay?" Langley asked when Oliver joined the rest of the team and immediately went back to checking his equipment.

"Yeah. Everything's fine." He was going to enjoy this last jump with his team, then speak with Hawk about a change of duty until Selena came through delivery and treatment.

He needed to have his mind in the game a hundred and ten percent if he was to do justice for the other guys in his team. And as long as Selena was going through this, he couldn't guarantee he'd be able to do it.

The rest of the men were already changing into thermal shirts to go under their polypropylene garments. It could get damn cold at twenty-nine thousand feet at the 126 mph they'd be dropping. They'd wait to put on balaclava face masks and gloves when they were airborne.

An hour and a half later, when they finally boarded the aircraft, they were weighted down with the rest of their gear, including body armor, an oxygen system and mask which snapped to his helmet, plus altimeter, parachute, and goggles. This time, he thought, they at least would not have the extra hundred pounds of equipment usually strapped to them during missions. Which meant more freefall time before he opened his chute.

"You wouldn't believe it. I've never caught a dolphin fish any bigger than twelve to fourteen pounds. This sucker had to be at least thirty," Doc said.

"This is beginning to sound like one of those tall tales you fishermen spin all the time," Sizemore said, the flash of his smile bright white in the dim light of the fuselage.

"I have proof." Doc dredged his iPhone from the right front pocket of his cammies with some difficulty. He scanned through the pictures until he came across the one he wanted. He held it up.

"You know pictures can be deceiving," Bowie said from his seat next to Doc. "Depending on the perspective."

The look of betrayal on Doc's face was almost comical. "Just for that, neither one of you guys are invited to my fish grill. I have enough mahi-mahi fillets to feed the entire team. We'll be eating and partying while you two sit home alone and hungry."

Oliver laughed, then just as quickly sobered. He was going to miss the guys. They were his backup down range, and had shown their support more times than he could ever repay.

"Hey, Greenback." Doc waved a hand to get his attention. He wandered over to where the guys had congregated. "We've been talking about nicknames. We know why Bowie got his, being from Texas. And mine is self-explanatory, as is Bullet's. But none of us know where yours came from." His brows rose. "Care to share and put the mystery to bed?"

Oliver braced a hand against the steel fuselage. He grinned at the memory the question triggered. "I had just made it through BUD/S, and we'd transported out to Machen to do SQT (SEAL Qualification Training). We were sent out to do some night maneuvers in the desert. You know, using compass and the stars to navigate and do patrols. Our lieutenant notifies us we have another team lying in wait to ambush us somewhere out there, and part of the fun is for us to avoid capture and get back to the base undetected. He assigned me and two others to protect our back door in case they approached us from the rear. It's black as pitch with a slice of moon the width of a gnat's eyelash, so we're wearing our NVGs so we can see two feet in front of us and not step on a rattlesnake or each other."

Doc and Bullet nodded a shared understanding in their expression.

"Well, the lieutenant radios back to check on us every so often, and I'm looking through the NVGs turning everything green in front of me, and every time he asks for a status I say, "It's green back here."

The men started to chuckle.

"By the time we got back to base camp, my name had become Greenback."

Doc shook his head with a wide grin. "It's a much better story than the stuff I imagined."

Oliver bumped knuckles with him and wandered over to take a seat next to Hawk. "I need to talk to you about something."

Hawk nodded. "Okay." He frowned. "Selena okay?"

"So far. But I don't think she's telling me everything. She's twenty-two weeks along and the chemo's been hard and is only going to get harder. I think it might be time for me to request a temporary duty change until the baby is born. I need to be on the ground and closer to home right now."

Hawk nodded. "Understood. Captain Jackson and I discussed this a couple of weeks ago. Go in and see him tomorrow. I think he has something in mind for you."

It was a reassuring to know command had his back in this. "Thanks, Hawk."

Hawk's gray gaze remained on his face. "You know this doesn't mean you're breaking ties with us, with this team. We'll still be here when you're ready to come back. And we'll still be there for you and Selena until she's well."

Emotion gripped his throat, and he looked away. "We couldn't do it without all of you. Zoe and Trish, Clara and Tess. Since Selena's mom left, they've been dropping meals by, and taking Lucia for play dates. They're all amazing."

Hawk gripped his forearm in a moment of commiseration. "Selena would be doing the same for them."

"Strap in and prepare for takeoff," the pilot's voice came over the COM. The engines turned over and then roared as they taxied forward, making it impossible to talk.

At ten thousand feet they leveled off and everyone donned their balaclava face masks, helmets, positioned their goggles and went on oxygen to leach the nitrogen from their bloodstreams. The plane circled for forty-five minutes, climbing to an altitude of twenty-nine thousand feet before the cargo bay door opened and the pilot announced they'd reached their diving height. They rose as one and packed together in jump formation near the incline. As soon as the pilot announced they were over the jump area, Hawk signaled, moved forward, and leapt. They all followed him as they'd done a thousand times before, through training, into battle, down ropes, and even out the backs of planes.

The curve of the atmosphere looked like a convex lens along the horizon, and the sound of the wind filled Oliver's ears despite his helmet. Up here at what looked like the top of the world, his heart raced and he came alive. Hurtling toward the earth fed the adrenaline junkie in him.

But down below the woman who nurtured his unborn child was struggling. He could do without this for a time. Until she was well.

At thirty-five hundred feet he deployed his chute. Air filled it and jerked him upward. He grasped the wooden handles used to manipulate the direction of descent. Below him Hawk's chute moved east, and he looked over his shoulder to locate the men behind him, and saw their chutes staggered in a landing formation, one above the other, following him down. His throat tightened with emotion.

Hawk was right. Nothing could break the ties between him and this team. When age or some physical condition made him unable to do this job, he'd still be tied to this life, and the men who lived it with him. He'd lived a lifetime in the five years he'd been a SEAL. He planned to live many more.

Selena was going to get well and he'd come back to his team.

CHAPTER EIGHT

S ELENA TURNED THE key in the door, pushed it open, then stood back for Lucia to precede her into the house. Had she ever been this tired? Maybe it was just an aftereffect of her doctor's appointment. She couldn't think about it just now. She'd start screaming the way she had as soon as she'd gotten in the car.

When she made it to the couch she kicked her shoes off and slumped back against the cushions. Lucia sidled up to her and Selena lifted the straps of her backpack free and dropped it next to the couch. Lucia climbed up on the cushions next to her.

She'd been unusually silent since Selena had picked her up at daycare. "What's wrong, baby?"

"You're hair's all gone, Mommy."

The tremulous tone in her voice arrowed straight into Selena's heart. She should have taken Lucia's reaction into consideration before shaving off her hair. Why hadn't she? Because she was slipping. She couldn't think of everything, do everything she needed to do and try to deal with everyone else's needs when it was such an effort to deal with her own.

"Mommy took some medicine and it made my hair fall out. So I had it cut." She pulled her scarf free and ran a hand over her scalp. There was a small patch of stubble at the crown and at the nape of her neck, but the rest was gone. "It will grow back soon."

Lucia got up on her knees and ran her small hand over the top of Selena's head.

Selena looped her arms around her to hold her steady. "Would you like it if Mommy wore a wig?"

"Whassat?"

How to explain? "It fits on your head like a hat, but it's made of hair." She pushed herself free of the couch and offered Lucia her hand. They wandered down the hall to Oliver's small office. The space was actually a spare bedroom. Right now a large, heavy plastic storage unit was tucked in the corner where Oliver kept extra military gear, his personal sig and a twelve gauge he'd had as a boy. She automatically checked the cabinet door to make sure it was still locked before sitting down at the computer desk and opening the laptop. Lucia wiggled up onto her lap. As soon as the browser came up, Selena typed in WIGS.

A whole list of companies who created wigs or sold them came up. She clicked on the image listing at the top and pictures of wigs popped up, some on Styrofoam heads and others suspended in space.

"Which ones do you like?" Selena asked. She breathed in the combination of baby shampoo, crayons and the outdoors distinctive to her active child.

"Dat one." Lucia pointed to a bright pink wig made of synthetic fibers.

"You think I'd look good with pink hair?"

"Yes."

"Or do you think Lucia would look good in pink hair?"

A wide smile spread across Lucia's face. "Yes."

Selena laughed and gave her a hug.

"Does my hair have to fall off?" Lucia asked.

"No." God forbid her baby would sink her teeth into the idea. She'd cut it off herself to hurry things along. "Mommy doesn't want your hair cut. I think it looks beautiful just as it is." Selena curled a long, shoulder-length strand around her finger to form a barrel curl. "But you can wear a wig over your hair if you want to."

"If Mommy gets a wig, Lucia will have to have a pink one," Oliver said from the door.

"Daddy!" Lucia wiggled free of her lap and ran to him. He swung her up into his arms. "Mommy's hair is all gone," she announced in a whisper.

"I see. She looks beautiful, doesn't she?"

Lucia turned to look over her shoulder. "Like the Moon Lady."

"It's a Chinese folk tale she learned about at daycare," Selena explained. She walked over to Oliver to lean against him. "The lady isn't bald, but for some reason it's how Lucia imagines her."

Lucia shimmed down and went to the computer to look at the pictures again.

His lips skimmed Selena's eyelids and he lay his cheek against her bare head. "I brought a couple of movies home. One for Lucia and a few for us. I thought we'd have a family night."

"Okay."

"I'm cooking. Doc sent you some mahi-mahi. He caught a thirty-pound dolphin fish. Can you believe that?"

"I didn't know they got so big."

"Bowie and Bullet voiced some disbelief and Doc has uninvited them to his next fish grill."

She laughed. "You know he'll change his mind. He's a soft touch."

"They know it, too. But he thought you might like some before everyone else, as a treat."

"That was really nice of him." The guys were forever doing thoughtful things. "I'll call and thank him."

Oliver ran his hand over her bare scalp. "You look like Sinead O'Connor."

Selena smiled. "With an Italian nose."

"What's wrong with your nose? I think it's perfect." He kissed it. "Why don't you lie down and rest while Lucia and I cook?"

She nodded. She was sure Langley had warned him about her hair, giving him time to adjust before seeing her. But just once she wished he'd come straight out and say she looked like shit. She had dark circles under her eyes and, though she forced herself to eat, she had lost weight. She was just a bald baby bump.

How could Oliver be so supportive about everything else and not about the baby? She wanted to march into the kitchen and confront him, but exhaustion born from two hard knocks in one day dragged at her limbs, and she could hardly keep her eyes open. She had to tell Oliver, but the prospect was just too much for her right now.

She went into her bedroom and pulled the top cover down. She shed her dress, put on a T-shirt and shorts, and slipped beneath the comforter. She was asleep in moments.

She woke to the sound of the television in the living room with an overwhelming need to urinate. She bailed out of bed and went into the bathroom.

When she came out Oliver stood at the dresser, removing his watch.

What time is it?" she asked.

"Nearly ten. You were sleeping so soundly I didn't want to wake you. Lucia and I ate fish and watched *Finding Nemo*. I assured her we weren't eating clown fish or a tang."

Selena smiled. "How did you know what kind of fish Dory was?"

"We had to look it up before she'd eat."

Selena laughed.

"Are you hungry?"

"No." She slipped beneath the covers and pulled them up. She opened with the easier of two pieces of news. "I told my boss today I needed to take a leave of absence."

Oliver strode to the side of the bed and sat down on the edge next to her.

"We knew you'd have to eventually."

"I made a mistake on a big contract which could have cost the bank thousands, Oliver." She started to run her fingers through her hair to push it back and caught herself when she met the soft skin of her scalp. "If Diana hadn't caught it, I'd have probably been fired."

He rested his fingers against the exposed nape of her neck. "I'm sorry, *carina.*"

"I should have discussed it with you, but—I couldn't take the risk of being fired. At least this way I might have a chance of going back." So why did it feel like such a defeat?

"It'll be okay, Selena. It was the right thing to do." He remained silent for a moment. "I talked to Hawk today about a change of duty so I can stay more available. He said Captain Jackson already had something for me. I'm seeing him tomorrow."

They were both losing out on important bits of who they were.

"I'm sorry, Oliver."

"It's just temporary for us both, Selena. As soon as you have the baby, and get well, everything will go back to normal."

No it wouldn't. Nothing would ever go back to the way it was before cancer. Their new normal was going to be something else entirely. "The doctor talked to me about what he called another measure of defense." She closed her eyes against the pain. "They want to take out my ovaries once the baby's born. I'll never have another child."

"Two will be enough, honey."

"I'll be thrown into menopause at twenty-eight. I'll have to stay on medication for ten years to make sure the cancer doesn't come back."

"Whatever it takes, Selena."

He clearly didn't understand what she was saying. Everything that made her a woman was being ripped away, one piece at a time. "My sex drive will be gone, Oliver. What if I can't want you anymore?"

He took her into his arms. "You promised me, and yourself, you would fight. Whatever it takes. As long as you survive, we can work on everything else. As long as you survive." His expression was fierce, intent.

She rested her cheek against his shoulder. If only she had his strength.

"If I lost an arm, a leg, you'd still love me, wouldn't you?" he asked.

"Yes." Her arms tightened around him.

"This is the same. These things don't make up the person you are. Your ovaries aren't what make you my Selena."

But it was part of what made her a woman. Because of all the hormones coursing through her, they couldn't be certain the chemo was slowing or stopping the spread of the cancer. The lymph node swelling under her right arm never went away, though she tried to keep the limb elevated as much as possible.

"You want to know what the sexiest thing about you is?"

"What?"

"Your laugh. It was the first thing I noticed about you in college. I'd gone to the party at Joe Rollins house, and the place was packed. Some babe in tight jeans and a barely-there top was putting the moves on me. And I should have been raring to go, since I was just one big hormone then, but I kept hearing your laugh.

"Finally I just walked away from the babe and followed the sound to the kitchen. You were there with a group of girls. You looked like you'd just graduated from Catholic high school. Fresh-faced, young, and less underdressed than most of the other college freshmen there. I asked you to dance and spent the rest of the night trying to make you laugh. Every time I hear it, I get hard."

How could she not love him after that story? She kissed him, then said, "You're so full of it."

He laughed. "I'm serious."

He looked so earnest she had to believe him. She cupped his face in her hands and kissed him again, this time with feeling. "What movie was it you brought home for us to watch?"

"The guys made a list and I got all the ones I was able to find."

If his team had made the list she could hardly wait to see what they'd chosen. "Go get them and we'll pop one in."

She drew a deep breath after he left the room. The tight feeling of pain and frustration had eased, and she was actually able to smile when he came back in. He fanned the stack of DVDs out on the bed. For a moment she was stunned, but then dissolved into a fit of the giggles.

Every movie had a bald heroine: *Alien 3, Empire Records, V for Vendetta, G. I. Jane* and *Star Trek: The Motion Picture.*

"Let's watch *G.I. Jane*," she suggested.

"You don't have to choose one you think I'd like. Contrary to popular belief, military operators do watch things besides war movies."

"I need to watch someone who's ready to kick butt."

He grinned. "Okay." He sauntered over to the small entertainment center angled in the corner of the room, popped in the DVD, and turned on the television. "You want some popcorn?"

She shook her head.

He shucked his shorts and slid beneath the covers in his boxer briefs and T-shirt. She cuddled close against his side and felt the baby move.

She was entitled to a few meltdowns. But she had to keep a positive attitude. The mistake at work, her hair loss, the chemo, the doctor's strong suggestion about her ovaries, and worry over the baby—they had all combined to knock her off her feet.

If adversity knocks me down, I will get back up. I will never give up the fight.

The opening credits of the movie rolled forward and she tried to lose herself in the story. At the point, when Demi Moore was doing sit-ups while hanging from a top bunk, Selena slipped her hand into Oliver's boxer briefs and curled her fingers around his penis. He hardened in an instant and a smile curved her lips.

He shifted to look down at her, his brown eyes already darkening with desire. "I thought we were watching a movie."

"We are watching a movie. But I've been asleep for hours and I'm feeling rested and...ready for something more."

He eyed her, his expression serious, as his hand moved beneath her T-shirt and he palmed her growing baby bump. "Are you sure it's okay?"

He might have freaked out about the baby because of her diagnosis, but his protective concern made her smile. His need to keep his distance was constantly at war with his paternal instincts. He might fool himself, but he couldn't fool her. Once the baby was born, he'd be as loving to it as he was to Lucia. She knew he would.

Her hand covered his. "It's okay."

He reached for the television control and turned it off.

She smiled. One of the best things about making love with her husband was on the way he paid attention to detail. He spent at least a decade kissing her, though she wanted to rush toward other things. She finally peeled his shirt up and he got the message and tossed it aside, then wiggled free of his briefs. The spiraling pattern of hair on his chest was soft beneath her hands. His nipples tightened while she toyed with them and tasted the salty heat of his skin. He shuddered in response and caught his breath.

In return, his hand fished beneath her T-shirt and found her left breast and caressed and toyed with the nipple. She had never allowed him to see the area where her right breast had been for fear it would crush any sexual feelings he had for her. But she reveled in the sensation when he touched her.

If he could still want her without a breast, without hair, maybe they would survive cancer as a couple. She trailed her lips to his collarbone and then nipped his shoulder while she looped her knee over his hip and moved against him.

"You're very impatient," he complained. "And you still have your shorts on."

"Carpe diem," she murmured into his ear and sucked on his earlobe.

He groaned and tugged her shorts down and off. There was a tremor in his arms as he moved up over her to wedge himself between her thighs, and she smiled at his excitement. His muscle-hardened stomach brushed hers distended with child. With one slow glide he thrust into her. The pleasure of their bodies joining, being as close as they could get, was both a joy and a relief.

He balanced his weight on his hands, careful not to put too much pressure on her. His slow, easy movements were somehow more sensual because of the care he showed her and because his position allowed her to watch his expression. With every gentle thrust her pleasurable tension built. She let it come, hoping to extend the moments of intimacy for as long as they could last. Oliver's expression of concentration morphed into a frown as he fought against his release. He reached down between them and touched her where their bodies joined, messaging the sensitive area until the slow-growing wave became a tsunami which broke over her and swept him along in its wake.

With the release came a fresh wave of exhaustion. She looped an arm around his neck and drew his lips down to hers for a long, sweet kiss. "I'm going to pretend I'm a man and roll over and go to sleep," she said, her voice breathy.

"I feel so used," Oliver said in an aggrieved tone.

She laughed. "If you want to turn the movie back on and finish it, it won't bother me." She caressed his cheek.

"Okay."

When she turned on her side, he moved to spoon with her, but didn't turn the light off. "I love you, Oliver."

"Ti amo per l'eternità," he said in return.

OLIVER CONTINUED TO hold her until her breathing deepened and slowed. He studied the fragile curve of her cheek, and the slender bridge of her nose. There was a new fragility to her shape, despite her pregnancy, which concerned him. She needed to eat more, for herself and the baby. No matter what kind of job he was assigned on post, from now on he was going to make it his calling to see she ate and slept as she should.

She could only fight effectively if she was in top form. And he was going to make some calls to her doctors and find out if there were things she wasn't sharing with him. He needed to know.

And maybe with a plan of action in place, he could keep the worry at bay.

CHAPTER NINE

SELENA RUBBED THE side of her swollen belly where tiny toes or fingers poked between her ribs with insistent determination and then pushed downward. If she were trapped in such a tight space, she'd probably be tempted to do the same.

She tensed at the sound of approaching footsteps. The curtain parted and Judy Elmer, one of the nurses, stepped into the alcove with a tray in her hand.

"Hey, Selena. Good to see you," Judy greeted her with a smile and set the tray on the table next to her. Her gaze dropped to Selena's belly. "It looks like your little one is progressing just as he should. Well, he or she."

"Yes. Dr. Sanderlin says the baby's almost nineteen inches long and weighs about six pounds."

"So you're going old school and don't know what you're having?" Judy asked.

"We want to be surprised. But Lucia, our three year old, has decided her/his name should be Gumby."

Judy laughed.

Selena gripped the arms of the recliner as the nurse peeled back her lapel to expose the port running into the vein just below her collarbone. Judy picked up a syringe filled with clear fluid and pulled loose the cap. "I'm just going to check your port for any blockage."

Selena nodded and closed her eyes while the nurse inserted the needle into the port and pushed the plunger. Though the process wasn't painful she held her breath.

"Everything's clear here. I'll check your vitals, then hook you up, okay?"

Selena swallowed though her mouth was dry. "Okay."

Judy took her pulse and blood pressure.

"You're blood pressure's a little high. Why don't we wait just a few minutes and see if it comes down?"

"Okay."

"Go ahead and just raise the footrest on the recliner and relax. I'll be back in a few minutes to check it again."

Selena nodded and tugged her scarf forward a little and smoothed it.

Judy stepped out of the curtained area and walked away.

She'd been told repeatedly the chemicals wouldn't hurt the baby, but her fear kicked in every time.

Everything she did these days was for one child or the other, and poor Oliver got neglected in the crunch. Even sex had been put on hold until after the birth.

He seemed just as focused, had been for months, on making sure she was eating healthy and unstressed. He messaged her swollen arm when lymphedema kicked in and bandaged it for her to keep the swelling down. He was all about her. While she ate, slept, breathed for the baby.

At thirty-five weeks, her maternal instincts were cranked to overdrive. She just needed this one thing to go right.

Judy returned a few minutes later with the bag of Saline and a smaller bag of fluid. She hooked the two together so the saline would feed the chemo into her port a little at a time.

She paused to take Selena's blood pressure again. "It's come down a little. Let's wait a few more minutes.

She left again and Selena tilted the recliner back, stared the ceiling, and wished Oliver were there to calm her. She closed her eyes and concentrated on breathing in and out.

Twenty minutes later Judy slipped back through the curtain.

She took a blood sample from the port and once again took her blood pressure. Judy recorded the reading and nodded. "I'll get your chemo started."

Selena rested her hands on her belly, holding it while Judy started the infusion. Once the needle was in place and the liquids were dripping, Judy pulled the curtains back so all the nurses could watch over her and Selena could socialize with the other patients if she wanted.

If only she could sleep through the next four hours, but the constant back and forth of the nurses, and knowing where she was, kept her from being able to relax.

Five other women sat in recliners in similar positions, all hooked up to IVs of one kind or another. When she'd begun the treatments, there had been as few as three and as many as ten other patients at any given time. She recognized a couple of the women and raised a hand in greeting.

"How many does this make for you?" the woman directly across from her asked.

"Treatments or children?" Selena asked.

"Both." The woman said.

"Six treatments, two children."

"Congratulations on both."

"Thanks." The painful tightening of her stomach muscles sent a wave of anxiety through Selena. It was just a Braxton Hicks contraction. She was fine. She'd be hyper-aware of every small twinge of discomfort until the baby was born.

She forced herself to concentrate, to keep talking with the woman across from her. "How many for you?" Selena asked.

"This is my seventh and final treatment."

"I'm so happy for you," Selena said with feeling. She was. And envious. Once the baby had arrived, she still had months of other therapies and surgeries to look forward to.

One thing at a time. As Oliver said.

She shifted in her seat as her back began to ache and once again a contraction hit.

She glanced toward the desk in search of Judy, but an unfamiliar nurse stood there recording something on a tablet. She watched the clock, only half listening to the conversation between the woman and another she also recognized. Five minutes later, when another spasm hit, she timed it.

Braxton Hicks didn't last sixty seconds and hurt like a son-of-a-bitch. Her heart rate soared and she couldn't catch her breath. She looked down the wide aisle to the desk and pushed the call button. It was too soon. The baby needed the extra five weeks to grow and develop.

Judy hurried over, "What is it, Selena?"

She tried to keep her voice calm but her words came out breathy and weak. She wasn't ready, the baby wasn't ready. "I'm in labor."

"BACK INTO THE surf, get wet and sandy," Oliver yelled. Eighty-two extremely tired men ran toward the water and rolled around in the surf, then returned to the sand and tumbled around in it until they were covered from head to toe.

Five minutes later he was yelling again. "Chainey! Do I see a dry spot on your shirt?"

"Hooyah, Ensign Shaker." The recruit who stood before him was six inches taller, at least forty pounds heavier, and looked about fourteen.

"Get your ass back in the surf and get sandy. And when I say get sandy, I mean every inch of you. The devil's in the details, Chainey. Every detail you miss on a mission can cost your life or someone else's."

"Hooyah, Ensign Shaker." The kid ran back into the ocean and allowed the water to flow over him, then he raced back to the loose sand twenty feet inland and rolled like a log. When he stood, he looked like the sugar cookie he should have resembled to begin with.

"Now give me twenty, Chainey, and do it quick because you're holding up your boat crew. You're putting their lives at risk because you are keeping them in a holding pattern while you take care of bullshit."

"Hooyah, Ensign Shaker." Chainey hit the sand. He counted out the twenty, leapt to his feet, and dashed over to join his boat crew, who stood holding the IBS—inflatable boat, small—aloft as instructed.

The summer surf crashed behind them as eight teams of eight men ran in a shuffle down the beach, their rubber boats balanced over them, and then back again. The breeze coming off the water was stiff. The surf was high and was going to give the boat crews a pounding.

It was the first day of BUD/S and they were weeding out the weak, the ones who didn't have the right mindset to make it through. There was a method to the torture they dished out, a learning curve to every exercise.

He was having a blast, though he kept his facial expression stern.

Oliver noticed a man dressed in shorts and the brown T-shirt worn by the instructors jogging toward them at a steady clip. He narrowed his eyes in an attempt to identify him. It was Seaman Corey Bryant, and Oliver frowned until the man changed course and started toward him. Oliver heart clenched and he sprinted to meet him.

"The hospital called. Your wife's gone into premature labor, during her chemo. She's been taken to maternity. I'm here to relieve you."

Oliver didn't stop to thank him, but broke into an all-out run up the beach to the facility. He was out of breath and shaking by the time he made it to his locker. He ignored the change of clothes and just grabbed his wallet and car keys.

It was just five weeks early. The baby would be fine. Selena would be fine. He'd been telling himself that for months. But what if they weren't? If something happened to the baby, Selena wouldn't be able to handle it. She'd clung to it as a ray of hope during a time of fear, and if it was suddenly taken from her—what then?

He pulled out of the parking lot and wove his way toward the front gate. He had to force himself to watch the speed limit, the urge to floor the gas pedal almost irresistible.

And what about him? How would he feel should his son or daughter's life be snatched away before it had a chance to begin?

He'd been tortured by both pain and guilt since the moment he'd suggested aborting the baby during their first doctor's appointment. If something happened to the baby now, it would be as though he'd willed it. Willed it with his need to keep his distance, in case it happened because of the cancer, the chemo, or just plain bad luck.

Would Selena forgive him for those words, spoken out of fear for her? He'd never asked her forgiveness. Never reneged on the intent behind them. Why hadn't he done so?

He shook with the need to be there at the hospital as he pulled up at the gate and was waved through by the MPs.

It seemed an eternity passed before he turned onto Bob Wilson Drive and saw the hulking shape of the Naval Medical Center. Then he faced the nightmare of trying to find parking.

SELENA TOOK DEEP breaths to steady her racing heart. The room in the maternity wing was empty but for her and the doctor. Thank God. Though the nurses had tried not to stare while she'd changed from her street clothes to a hospital gown, the sight of her mastectomy scar had given them both pause. But it had gotten them on the phone to her ObGyn probably more quickly than otherwise.

"You have to calm down, Selena," Dr. Sanderlin said, her voice steady. "The baby's fine. You're fine. We're giving you something to lower your blood pressure.

"Did someone call Oliver?" Would she ever be able to do anything again without turning to Oliver for reassurance? Since quitting her job, she'd turned into a dependent ninny.

"Yes, they've called him, and I'm sure he's on his way."

"Can we stop the labor? Wouldn't it be better if we waited a few more weeks?"

"Every week is important, but you were already dilated three centimeters at your last visit and you're at six now. I don't think trying to stop your labor is the right thing to do. It will put your body and the baby under more stress. And leave you open to infection. I think our best option is to let nature take its course.

"I've ordered a test on the amniotic fluid we withdrew just a few minutes ago," Dr. Sanderlin continued. "It should be back within the hour. The neonatal intensive care unit will be prepared if there's any issue with lung development. But I just looked at the fetal development on your ultrasound and everything looks fine. He's just going to be small."

Another contraction hit and Selena tried to breathe with it. She had done this alone last time. She could do it again if she had to. But she really wanted Oliver. The unbearable feeling of pressure in her lower abdomen seemed to go on forever. She had to turn on her side to grip the bar on the hospital bed. When it eased, she drew a cleansing breath.

"I have to lie on my side. I can't lie flat on my back."

"You can lie in whatever position is most comfortable, Selena." Dr. Sanderlin laid a reassuring hand on her shoulder. "The baby's turned in the right direction. Everything is going to be fine. You're doing great."

The baby's steady heartbeat through the monitor reassured her all was right with him/her.

"I've already called down to anesthesia and the nurse will be up to give you an epidural. I've already placed the order in your chart. I'm not expecting any problems, but I'd prefer you had one just in case."

"Okay."

"I'm going to send a nurse midwife in to sit with you until your husband gets here. When you get close to delivery I'll be back." Dr. Sanderlin left the room and Selena closed her eyes and geared up for the next contraction. It was already building.

OLIVER RAN FROM the parking structure to the hospital. Inside the place proved to be a maze, and the longer it took him to find the maternity wing the more his anxiety escalated. When he finally found the door, he had to be buzzed in by one of the nurses.

She handed him a gown to cover up with, then pointed out the room. He jogged to it and pushed open the door. A strange woosh-woosh-woosh sound came from a monitor by the bed. Selena gripped the bar next to her in obvious pain. A blonde woman stood close, offering her encouragement.

The sight of his wife in pain hammered him with a one-two punch. Seeing her curled on her side in a hospital bed, her scalp bare, gave him visions of something worse. His breathing stopped as he absorbed the roundhouse blow. He'd run toward danger his whole SEAL career, but nothing had scared him more than seeing her like this. It was a nightmare he'd done everything to avoid, to help *her* avoid.

Her eyes focused on him. "Oliver."

The sound of her voice broke the spell.

She needed him. This was the birth of their child. It had nothing to do with the cancer.

The first step was the hardest, but once he'd made it, his feet moved forward on their own. He hooked a nearby chair and jerked it close to the bed, his breathing coming in unsteady gasps. He made an effort to slow it, and then leaned over the railing to press his lips to her forehead and run a comforting hand down her back. "How's it going?"

"My water just broke." She glanced over her shoulder at the blonde woman.

"My name is Sharon Rollins, I'm a nurse midwife here at the hospital," she said as she reached for rubber gloves from the bedside table.

He nodded. "Oliver."

She tipped her chin in acknowledgement. "I need to check you, Selena."

Selena rolled on her back and just as quickly rolled back. "Wait-wait."

The look of focused control on her face as she dealt with the pain reassured Oliver a little. She had done this before, knew what to expect. She'd done it *alone*. *Jesus!* His every muscle tensed with regret and sympathy. When she drew a breath, so did he.

The woman folded back the sheet and did an internal exam. "This baby's in a rush, you're at ten," she announced. "You're going to want to push, but try not to. Try and blow through it." She tugged off her gloves and pushed the paging button on the bed. When a voice answered she said, "Page Dr. Sanderlin, stat, and alert the NICU, they need to get someone down here *now*."

Selena grasped Oliver's wrist and her fingers dug in as she started to blow. "Please, please."

"What do you need me to do?" Oliver asked the nurse midwife.

"When the rest of the crew get in here, she'll want to hold on to you while she pushes." She raised the head of the bed, dropped the foot, helped Serena onto her back, and positioned her feet in the stirrups.

Seeing his wife so vulnerable and exposed, and so helpless to do anything about it, Oliver slipped an arm around Selena and held on through the next contraction.

Suddenly the room was filled with people. Selena's doctor strode in dressed in a gown and gloves.

"We didn't get the epidural, did we?" she said.

Selena just stared at her wide-eyed.

"It's okay. I don't think we'll need it. Let's have a baby."

Oliver had thought he knew what labor was until now. With every contraction, his wife pushed and pushed. He learned to count for her as she bore down, again and again. His arm ached where she clutched it. He blocked it out. The discomfort was nothing compared to what she was going through. Ten minutes turned into twenty. How could one small baby require so much effort to be born? Sweat rolled down his face and hers. A nurse wiped it away for them both.

"The baby's crowning, Selena. One more push."

Dr. Sanderlin had already said the same thing several times. He didn't believe it anymore.

"The head is out. Don't push, Selena. *Don't push.*" The doctor's voice held an edge. Her hands worked frantically below, doing something neither of them could see. Her frantic movements and her tone gripped Oliver by the throat.

"Push one more time, Selena. One last big one."

Her face lined with exhaustion, Selena dragged in one more breath and held it. Her grimace of effort scored deep lines around her eyes and mouth. The moment the baby slipped free he saw the relief in her face.

"It's a boy. Hurry—take him," Dr. Sanderlin said, passing a bundle wrapped in white cloth off to the NICU nurse standing by. She rushed the baby to the small hooded table and was joined there by two other medical personnel.

He barely heard Dr. Sanderlin when she said, "You're going to feel a little pressure, Selena."

The silence in the room stretched for an eon. Selena's gaze swung upward to him, panicked fear stretching her features into a mask. His arms tightened around her as a cry of pain and denial built in his chest.

A high-pitched squeal shattered the terrifying quiet, followed by a trembling cry. The entire room took a breath.

"Sounds like someone's mad," Dr. Sanderlin said, with a quick smile.

Tears streamed down Oliver's face. "I didn't mean what I said in your office the first day."

Dr. Sanderlin set her the medical instrument on the tray the nurse held out to her. "I know."

"I didn't mean it, Selena."

Selena turned her face into his chest and gripped his scrubs in her fists. "I know, Oliver. I've always known. It's okay. We're okay."

EPILOGUE

S ELENA DRIED HER sweaty palms on her pants legs while she
shivered from the doctor's office air conditioning. How many
trips to this office had she made in the last six months? At least
twenty. Not counting the trips for blood work, X-rays, mammograms, biopsies, all the procedures she'd been unable to have
before Micah's birth.

Oliver bounced and weaved in his daddy dance while he gave
the baby his bottle. Micah was her miracle baby. He'd not only
survived having the cord wrapped around his neck at birth—
something they only learned from Dr. Sanderlin after the heart-
numbing moment in her hospital room—but he'd also survived
the targeting chemo she'd needed while she carried him. He had
no lasting effects from either.

Following the birth she'd been bombarded with tests and procedures in a rush to knock out the cancer which had spread to her
liver, but not to her other breast. Then came radiation, more
chemo, and hormone suppression therapy, all of which she prayed
had done the trick. She'd had another MRI just this week and now
they were here to learn the diagnosis.

How many miracles could one person receive before God
said, "Sorry, but you've reached your quota?" All she needed was
one more.

Oliver settled Micah in his carrier, which was waiting on the floor between them, and handed him a set of plastic keys to chew on. He was teething, and he gnawed on the toy with quiet attention while he made a happy humming noise. She bent to put a cloth diaper beneath his chin to catch the slobber. He had Oliver's curly hair, just as Lucia did, and she curled a strand around her finger.

Oliver sat down beside her. She straightened and brushed her bangs back with her fingers, then clenched her hand into a fist in her lap to hide their trembling.

Oliver grasped her hand and laced their fingers. "The wig looks great—natural and sexy," Oliver said. "I like the short 'do on you." His smile would have looked natural to anyone else, but she noticed the tightness at the corners. He was as anxious as she was.

"I thought it looked more like a kick-ass heroine in an action movie. I'm getting well. I wanted to look the part." She had worked hard to regain some of her self-confidence and leave behind the clinging vine she'd become...even though Oliver repeatedly denied any evidence of it.

He bent to brush her knuckles with his lips. "Hooyah!" he said with feeling.

The door opened behind them and they both turned to look.

Dr. Sanderlin walked through first, but she wore no lab coat, and her hair was loose about her shoulders. She smiled at Selena, then Oliver. Dr. Dixon, tall, gray-haired and studious, followed.

Selena dragged air into her lungs, but her breath stuck in her throat. This was either very, very good or—She didn't want to think about it.

"I wanted to be included in this meeting," Dr. Sanderlin said. "Since it all started in my office nearly a year and a half ago, I asked Dr. Dixon if I could sit in."

The tight, anxious ball of nerves wedged beneath Selena's ribs began to ease.

Dr. Dixon cleared his throat. "There is no sign of cancer anywhere in your latest scans. Two other radiologists and I have gone over them. There's nothing there."

Selena's composure dissolved in relief and she covered her face with her hands and burst into tears.

Oliver pulled her to her feet and wrapped her in his arms. They clung, hard, and when she raised her face to him, he kissed her.

"We'll want you to stay on your regimen for a few more months before we switch you over to suppression therapy to maintain your status," Dr. Dixon continued. "You're ready for breast reconstruction now, whenever you feel up to it."

"I can give you a list of Board Certified plastic surgeons your insurance will cover," Dr. Sanderlin added.

A sound of joy, half laugh, half sob, broke from Selena. She'd have her breast back. She'd look like a healthy woman again. It's what she wanted. She left Oliver's arms to hug first Dr. Sanderlin, then Dr. Dixon.

"You did all the heavy lifting, Selena," Dr. Dixon said, patting her back.

"Not without Oliver," Selena said.

Dr. Sanderlin held Micah and admired his new tooth. Dr. Dixon loosened up and held him for a moment as well. They celebrated for a few more minutes, and then gathered Micah, the diaper bag, and returned to the van.

"We need to call everyone and give them the news," Selena said while she paced and watched Oliver strap the baby in and pull the door closed.

"Later, after we've celebrated a little on our own," Oliver said, flashing her a grin. He rested his arms on either side of her and leaned in, pushing her back against the van, and nestling his body in perfect alignment with hers.

Her heart raced and a small tingle settled in intimate areas. It took more effort these days to get her going, but Oliver was patient. At times it must have seemed almost as big a challenge to him as one of his missions. Thank God he was a SEAL. They never gave up.

He kissed her, then rested his cheek against hers.

As though he'd read her thoughts, he whispered, "Hawk once

told me I'd never break the ties I have to my team. And I thought, because of everything I'd been through with them, I'd never have as strong a bond with anyone else. But I was wrong.

"When you've shared a life-and-death struggle as we have, it either makes you cling to one another, or it breaks the ties between you." His brown eyes were liquid with love and emotion. "I know there have been times when things were stretched pretty thin between us, especially when I was acting like an ass at the beginning. But, every time, we've rebounded and our ties have just grown stronger. I'm so lucky, Selena. I could have lost you so many times, so many ways."

Her eyes filled and her lips trembled as she whispered, "When I couldn't fight for myself, you helped me fight for you, and Lucia, and Micah. When I believed I had nothing left, you showed me I did. I couldn't have survived this without you." She rested her cheek against his chest until her tears and shakes abated.

He pulled back an inch or two and ducked his chin so he could look right into her eyes. "And you know the saying, the only thing tougher than a Marine is his wife?"

She smiled up at him. "Yeah."

"Well those women ain't got nothin' on me and my girls."

THE END

BREAKING POINT

A SEAL TEAM HEARTBREAKERS NOVELLA

Teresa J. Reasor

DEDICATION

To all the social workers who put their time and hearts into the job of protecting and helping families, you are appreciated.

And to all the dedicated spouses who hold down the fort while their loved ones are deployed (my mother being one of them), my respect and admiration for you is boundless.

PROLOGUE

IRAQ, 2010

WIND FROM THE CH-46 helicopter's propellers pounded the ground and beat up a whirlwind of dust and debris. The chopper rose higher and higher. Nose tilted slightly down, it sped toward the northeast.

Chief Petty Officer Langley Marks watched it disappear into the darkness with a mixture of regret and frustration. If he hadn't landed wrong rappelling down a rope in an earlier mission, he'd be on board the chopper now, and on his way with the team.

Damn it.

The distinctive clatter of the Chinook's propellers churning the air grew fainter and fainter, until it dissipated completely.

Balancing his weight on the crutches, Langley swung around and headed back to the communications shed, where he'd monitor the team's progress until they returned to base. He wasn't fit for much else at the moment. His foot and ankle were a glorious purple beneath the ace bandage, and his bare toes matched. Even a sock hurt at this point.

Knowing he wouldn't be able to accompany the team, he'd spent his time reviewing the compiled satellite footage of the terrorists' movements in and around the building they were using as a makeshift armory, looking for weaknesses. He and the team had gone over and over every element of the mission. If all went well, they'd be back in a matter of hours.

But, damn it, he should be there with them, monitoring the tangoes' activities while Greenback guarded their back door. They needed someone keeping an eye out for trouble while the guys were wiring the place to go up.

Because of his clumsiness, they were a man down, which could seriously affect the mission. He'd encouraged Hawk to take a replacement, but he refused. The team had grown close during the past seven months, and now had a working rhythm so familiar they practically read each other's minds and anticipated moves.

Fuck.

Even the bounce of his forward momentum on the crutches made his ankle and foot ache. He was gritting his teeth by the time he made it to the cinderblock, flat-roofed communications and mission control hut.

Seaman Charles Archer, one of the radio techs, greeted him with a wave while he monitored radio traffic through his headphones.

"What's happening?" Langley asked as he joined him.

Archer pulled one of the ear pads away and tipped his head to ask Langley to repeat the question, then answered, "One of the patrols is late returning, and Samuels is monitoring in case of trouble. I'll be on the com with your team as long as they're out."

Lieutenant Walters, who stood next to Archer, was in charge of logistics for the mission. If they needed emergency extraction or air support, he'd be the one to make the call.

Walters gave a nod, acknowledging him. "Have a seat, Lang."

Langley sat down in a folding chair a couple of feet away from Archer and propped his foot on another.

Archer glanced up. "I haven't heard anything since the chopper left." A tendril of sweat ran down his cheek, and he hunched one shoulder to wipe it away with his sleeve. The radios put out quite a bit of heat, and while the fans placed around the room circulated the air, they did little to cool it.

"I'll hang out until they reach the drop site and get clear. Then they'll observe radio silence during the mission."

Archer nodded and went back to listening. "Roger, Mike-Romeo-seven-three." He smiled and looked up. "They've reached the drop site. Everything's quiet. The flight crew is on their way back."

It was quiet for now. Langley glanced at his dive watch. At zero four hundred every morning, the Taliban decided to shoot RPGs across the base perimeter. Thus far they only managed to hit a Humvee and a latrine. Luckily, no one had been inside the vehicle or the shitter at the time.

Every time they hunted for the assholes, they disappeared into the labyrinth of streets and alleys.

But the Taliban fucker's luck and their aim might improve. And that would be about the time Hawk and the team were scheduled to return to base.

Captain Morrow, the base commander, wandered in five minutes later, and Langley and Seaman Archer got to their feet.

"At ease, Chief, Seaman," Morrow motioned them back down. "Put the radio on open mike, Seaman Archer."

Archer flipped the switch immediately.

"I'll be sticking around for a while," the Captain announced.

Walters nodded while Kyle stayed alert for transmissions.

Morrow nodded toward Langley's foot. "How is it? I can see your toes are purple from here."

"It isn't broken, but it's going to take some time for the soft tissue to heal. Once the swelling goes down and I can get a boot back on, I'll be ready to go again."

Archer shot him a doubtful look over his shoulder.

Morrow pulled a folding chair over and sat down. Two more support staff showed up to man the radios next to them.

Time passed slowly. Every time Langley was tempted to pace, his foot reminded him he couldn't. He hated waiting. And they did a lot of that in the SEALs. Waiting for transport. Waiting to go into action. Waiting in line for things.

Waiting to go home. That was the worst. It was weighing on them all right now. They were so close to the end of their deployment, every day seemed an eternity. He wanted to see his kids and hold them. He wanted to be in the same room with his wife instead of on a computer screen talking to her, or on a telephone line that sounded like she was a million miles away, which she was.

He did this to himself. It was his fault they weren't together in one place longer than six months. And with all the training, often less.

His kids were growing up without him.

But he couldn't make himself walk away from his team. Couldn't turn his back on the loyalty to his team built from the blood, sweat, and tears they'd shed together. What they did was important. They saved lives. They protected people who couldn't defend themselves.

They took out bad guys, terrorists, who wouldn't think twice about killing themselves and their families, all in the name of power. They could say it was for their religion, but it wasn't. It boiled down to keeping their iron grip on what they claimed was theirs—their families, their women—because they were afraid if they didn't, their power would slip away, leaving them impotent.

They needed to grow a pair, man up for their families. Feed them instead of running around with guns, trying to kill anyone who didn't agree with them.

The little voice that said he wasn't doing all he needed to do for his own family was cut off when he heard "Strong Man," Derrick Armstrong, whisper over the radio, breaking the silence. "We have a problem. C's a no-show, over."

Hawk's voice came next. "Cutter, come in, over."

Dead silence answered him.

They had the building rigged to blow. The timers were counting down. Langley jerked to his feet, forgetting his ankle and foot, and winced at the pain. He braced a hand on the table holding the radio and bent at the waist.

"Last location, over," Hawk asked, his voice even, calm.

Strong Man replied, "Ground floor. I thought he was right behind me, over."

"Greenback," Oliver Shaker, cut in. "Five minutes."

Seconds ticked by like minutes.

Hawk's voice, resolute and flat, cut the silence. "I'm going back in for him, over."

Langley gripped the edge of the table. "Jesus."

Captain Morrow waved him down and placed a hand on his shoulder.

The next few minutes were agony. Langley rested his head on the flat edge of the table, his tension ratcheting up until he thought his bones might crumble to dust.

It was a lifetime before the next radio communication.

"Flash, what's your position?"

That sounded like Hawk. *Thank you, Jesus.*

"I'm a hundred feet east of your last position."

"Stay where you are, we're on our way."

"Movement from the east here," Greenback announced, and then after a few minutes, "Patrol coming at you."

Silence settled in. Nausea rolled over Langley. God, he should be there. Helping them. His whole team could be wiped out. *God, please don't let it happen.*

It was an agony of waiting. An hour passed, then thirty minutes more. No one spoke.

"This is Alpha-Bravo-four-niner requesting an air strike at these coordinates. The enemy is at our gates," Hawk sounded calm, but stressed. He was shouting over the sound of machine gun fire.

Walters gestured to one of the other radiomen. The man got busy calling up help. "Four minutes."

Archer relayed the message. "Alpha-Bravo-four-niner, help has been detoured to your location. ETA four minutes."

Langley recognized the coordinates. "That'll be right on top of them."

Jesus, four minutes could be like a day and a half when they needed it now. He wiped the sweat off his face with his arm.

Morrow moved restlessly, his thick gray hair gleaming the color of sheet metal under the dull lighting. His jaw worked, though he remained in his seat, his arms folded against his chest.

Nearly ten minutes passed before Hawk's voice came over the

radio.

"This is Alpha-Bravo-four-niner. Remaining targets are bugging out. We're ready for extract, but this will be a hot extract."

"Roger, Alpha-Bravo-four-niner."

"Be aware we have one man down with a head injury, and another with an injured knee. The head injury needs immediate evac to the medical facility."

Langley's heart settled somewhere in his stomach. Who was hurt? Was it Cutter?

"Roger, Alpha-Bravo-four-niner."

Five minutes later one of the Chinook pilots came over the radio. "This is Lima-Mike-two-three. We have two injured, one with a head injury, and request support teams in place at touchdown."

"Roger, Lima-Mike-two-three."

"It has to be Brett," Langley said aloud. "Something happened inside the building."

"We'll find out soon enough…in about forty minutes," Captain Morrow reached for his phone. "I'll call Corporal Landis to drive us over to medical. You won't make it over there on those crutches."

The lights around the medical facility glowed dull yellow, almost swallowed by the darkness. The air stirred lazily, cold and dry. Gunfire sounded in the distance. It never stopped.

The sound of the helicopter approaching was overwhelmed by the noise of an RPG exploding about four hundred yards downrange from the landing site.

There was a lull while the Chinook approached. They both looked up at the distinctive sound of an RPG firing again. Langley tensed, waiting for the blast. It hit two hundred feet away, kicking up dirt.

The chopper came in closer. Another RPG launched. It was slow motion while the rocket-propelled grenade almost skimmed the tail of the helo and dropped to the ground. Everyone below ducked as the grenade exploded and ripped a hole in the landing pad. The chopper jerked right and spun around, dust billowing, and smoke from the explosion swirling with it. The Chinook dropped straight down a hundred feet from the pad.

Alarms blared, and a water truck raced around the corner of the building while the loading ramp lowered.

"Why don't we figure out where that asshole is and take him out?" Langley yelled above the helicopter's noise.

"If you can find him, be my guest," Morrow yelled. "They have a weapon, and they're a threat to the base and a danger to our personnel."

Langley ground his teeth and nodded. "Consider it done."

Morrow's brows rose, and he glanced down at Langley's purple foot.

Langley gritted his teeth. He was sick of this shit. Two of his team were hurt. He couldn't do shit about that, but he could take care of this asshole so he couldn't hurt anyone. Or knock a chopper carrying wounded out of the sky.

Langley waited impatiently while the team with the gurney double-timed out to the Chinook. The urge to run out there himself was nearly overwhelming, but his throbbing foot dissuaded him.

Hawk's hulking six foot four frame hobbled toward them, finally reaching the dim light projected from the medical building behind them. Strong Man gripped the arm slung over his shoulders, supporting some of Hawk's weight. A corpsman rushed out with a wheelchair, and Strong Man lowered Hawk into it.

The crew wheeling the gurney sped past them with "Doc," Zach O'Connor, in their wake. "Cutter," Brett Weaver, lay still and pale on the board, a bandage wrapped around his head to keep it stationary. A bruise the width and length of a large hand discolored his temple all the way down to his cheekbone, and he had an IV in his arm. He didn't look good.

Hawk hobbled up. "Mine's just a sprain. Doc's staying with Brett, giving them info. Maybe the doctors will share something after they've examined him. The rest of the team is going to secure our weapons and gear."

"Corporal Landis can drop them off," Captain Morrow said.

Hawk motioned to Greenback, Bowie, Strong Man, and Flash, who were laden with their weapons and packs as well as Doc's, Cutter's, and Hawk's. They headed for the Humvee and piled in. The vehicle pulled out.

Langley and Captain Morrow followed Hawk into the hospital and down the hall. Morrow joined Hawk in the exam area curtained off for triage. A doctor and nurse went into the small cubicle.

Brett was only in the cubicle a few minutes when two nurses wheeled him right back out and down a hall, double-timing it, with Doc following behind them.

Langley wandered up and down the hall on his crutches, restless, anxious. Twenty minutes later Doc trudged back down the hall, his pack still hanging on his back, his freckled face pale beneath a coat of grime. "He has a subdural hematoma and is in surgery. They're drilling a hole in his skull to relieve the pressure."

"Jesus!" Langley muttered, and a queasy feeling attacked him. He swallowed against it. "Is he going to live?"

"Once they relieve the pressure on his brain and get him stabilized... They won't know for several days. They won't know how much damage has been done to his brain until he wakes up. If he wakes up. We were out there for what seemed like a lifetime. I could tell one of his pupils was sluggish, so I knew it wasn't just a severe concussion. He never showed any signs of consciousness. All I had to give him for inflammation and swelling was hydrocortisone. That's like treating a bullet wound with a Band-Aid." Doc ran his fingers through the thick ruff of hair that hung down on his forehead, and his eyes grew glassy.

Langley gripped his shoulder and gave it a squeeze. "You did the best you could, using everything you had to work with. No one could ask any better of you, Doc. You kept him going until you got back here."

He nodded, but closed his eyes for several moments, his struggle for composure obvious. "They'll probably evac him to Germany as soon as he's stable."

Jesus! Langley leaned back against the wall. Just yesterday, while he elevated his foot, he'd watched the guys play touch football to blow off some steam. They didn't have anything close to a real field, but had chosen a spot just behind the cinderblock barracks. Other team members and a few Marines had joined in the game. Brett had quick reflexes, and intercepted the ball a couple of times. And he ran the ball into the end zone for a touchdown both plays.

What if he couldn't walk or speak? What if he never woke up? *Dear God.*

If only he had been there. Being with them to back up the team might have prevented this. Guilt bombarded him.

The two of them wandered down the hall to triage to find Captain Morrow in the waiting area. "Any news?"

Doc repeated what he knew. Morrow's expression was grave when he gave Doc the same pep talk he'd just heard from Langley. When the Captain started to leave with Doc in tow, Langley said, "I'm staying for awhile."

Morrow nodded. "Keep me posted."

"I will. Thanks, Captain."

The large triage area, which was divided by curtains that created twelve-by-ten cubicles on each side of a wide middle aisle, took up three-quarters of the large, open room. On the way back, Langley passed several medical personnel, and two nurses asked if he'd been taken care of. After a brief exchange, he clomped his way down the aisle and glanced into the curtained areas on both sides until he found Hawk.

Langley swung through the curtain. Hawk's dark hair hung in sweat-dampened strands on either side of his face. His tanned skin looked pale with pain. His pants leg was split up the outer seam, exposing a knee swollen to the size of a soccer ball.

Langley grimaced in sympathy. "They taking you to X-ray?"

"Yeah, in just a few minutes."

"They give you something for pain?"

"Yeah. It's starting to kick in."

"Good. You need anything?"

"No. Not right now. Just sitting here is good."

There was a look they all got when they'd been on a particularly dangerous mission. It was a mixture of relief and exhaustion, but also a kind of numbness crept in after the adrenaline high crashed.

"Long fucking night, listening to you guys on the radio and not being there to help."

"Be glad you weren't. Longest fucking night I've spent since being in the teams. It got pretty hairy several times, especially at the extraction site. Those flyboys really know their stuff, though. Otherwise we wouldn't be here talking. We were in the middle of a field with ordinance going off all around us, so close all we could do was stay curled in a ball and hold on to one another."

Langley rested a hand on Hawk's shoulder. Of all his teammates, he was closest to Hawk. He was one of the bravest men he knew, but right now he looked shocky. "Do you know what happened to Cutter?"

Hawk remained silent for a long moment. He beckoned Langley to come closer. Lang balanced on his good leg and set aside the crutches, then braced a hand on the metal headboard and leaned close. "He was stuffed behind a cabinet in the room he had wired. What kind of terrorist attacks an intruder, doesn't alert the others, and shoves his body behind a cabinet so he isn't found before the detonation?"

A prickling rush of shock rushed through Langley's limbs. He jerked up and met Hawk's gray gaze. Not a terrorist. One of their team tried to kill Brett Weaver.

CHAPTER ONE

SAN DIEGO, 2016
SATURDAY, 6:00 a.m.

TRISH MARKS FLUFFED her cap of straw-blond hair. This style would be easier to take care of than the longer one she'd worn forever. It was time for a change. She always ended up tying it back in a ponytail to keep it out of the way anyway. And it was just hair. If she decided she didn't like it, she could grow it back.

Too bad it didn't make her feel any lighter.

There was a weight dragging on her. The position of it didn't register. She just knew it felt like she was being driven slowly, relentlessly into the ground.

The weight of taking care of too many cases at work. The weight of the kids and all their activities, in school and out. The weight of the household, the yard work, the cooking, cleaning—everything.

Sometimes when she lay in bed at night, with the empty spot beside her where Langley should be, her heart started pounding louder and louder, and she couldn't catch her breath because of that density pressing down on her.

The weight of having her husband deployed and in danger hurt the most. At least that particular issue was lifted somewhat. Langley was finally home. But he wasn't entirely. Not yet.

They were going through a longer than usual adjustment period. And part of it was her fault. She was feeling ragged out, stressed, and just plain resentful. She'd spent a lot more time in the bathroom talking herself out of biting his head off this time, too.

Langley was patient with her. Too patient. She wanted them to have a screaming row, but instead they were silent because of the kids. Maybe if they hammered at each other with words it would end this heavy, stifling feeling.

Especially right now, with Langley getting ready to leave for a two-week training. He just got back from a deployment, and his three weeks of leave hadn't been long enough for them to put their family back together. And they'd exchanged some sharp words in the past few days.

After fifteen years of marriage, she'd learned to deal with everything alone. But lately, with the added caseload heaped on everyone at the office, she couldn't seem to get her feet under her.

What was *wrong* with her? Why was she struggling so?

Because her husband was gone more than half the year, and her son was acting out because he felt neglected by the one parent whose approval and attention he needed most.

"Tad, stop it." Jessica's voice, strident and sharp, carried down the hall interrupting Trish's thoughts.

Like fingernails down a blackboard. Were there still blackboards in schools? She hadn't seen any in the classrooms she visited in the last few years. They'd all gone to white boards or smart boards.

"Taaaaadd."

Trish slipped on her shoes, went to the door, and looked down the hall. Tad's shadow, elongated and skinny, was projected against the wall opposite Jessica's bedroom door. Trish started down the hall.

"You took my picture while I was practically naked, you little shit." Her twelve-year-old son's irate tone was worrying, and Trish lengthened her stride, instinctively knowing things were escalating.

"I'm sick of you wandering into my bedroom any time you want. It's my room. When the door is closed, stay out."

Trish reached the door just in time to see him raise the small camera Jessica got for her birthday two weeks earlier, and spike it down to the floor like it was a football and he just made a touchdown. She heard the crack of the device breaking at the same moment Jessica cried out. Her features were already crumpling as she rushed to pick up the camera.

Shocked at the violence of his reaction, the willful destruction, Trish stared at him. When she found her voice she only managed, "Tad—"

Anger still had a grip on him, and he shoved past her, stomped down the hall to his room, and slammed the door.

Jessica dropped to the floor and cradled the camera against her. Her heartbroken sobs gave Trish's own heart a hard pinch. Her daughter had been asking for a camera of her own for a year. The camera, the only thing she'd wanted for her birthday, was now her prized possession, and she'd been so careful with it.

A small bit of plastic, part of the housing, crunched beneath Trish's foot when she stepped into Jess's room, and she flinched. The camera couldn't stand up to Tad's rage. That, too, gave her heart a jab.

She crossed to her eight-year-old daughter, sat down on the floor, and gathered Jessica close. She rocked her and smoothed her dark brown hair back from her forehead, but managed to resist joining in with a few sobs of her own, though her eyes stung and her throat ached. Twenty minutes passed before Jessica's crying subsided into hitched breaths.

"Tad will be responsible for buying you a new camera."

Jessica used her T-shirt to wipe her nose. "It won't be the same."

No. Trish didn't think it would. It wasn't the loss of the camera. It was her brother's conscious desire to hurt her that Jessica would remember.

"I deleted the picture, but Tad wouldn't listen." Fresh tears streamed down her face. "He hates me."

"No, he doesn't. He's just going through some changes because he's getting older. He doesn't want me in his room when he's dressing either. Do you know what it means when I say you invaded his privacy?"

Jessica nodded. "It means I opened the door while he was dressing and I shouldn't have."

"Promise me you won't do that again."

Jess's chin wobbled, and more tears streamed down her cheeks. "I won't." She turned her face into Trish's shirt, another sob escaping.

She was such a sensitive child. She rarely did anything demanding discipline. The harshness of Tad's actions would stay with her for a long time.

The uncontrolled rage in his expression would stay with Trish.

She got to her feet and went into the bathroom across the hall to get some tissues and a wet washcloth.

When she returned, Jessica was sitting on the bed. She'd placed the camera on the nightstand, but her eyes still rested on it while slow tears continued to run down her cheeks and drip off her chin.

Trish offered her the Kleenex first. After she made good use of it, Trish wiped her face with the washcloth. "Why don't you lie down and rest for a few minutes while I go talk with your brother?"

Jessica curled on her side on top of her colorful comforter decorated with cats of all shapes and sizes. Her dark hair clung to her cheeks from sweat, tears, and the washcloth. Trish smoothed it back and pressed a kiss to her forehead.

She picked up the camera from the nightstand, went down the hall to Tad's room, tapped on the door, and waited a moment before opening it.

Tad was slouched in a molded plastic chair she'd just bought him, his large feet propped on the footboard of the bed. He was twelve but could easily pass for thirteen or fourteen because of a recent growth spurt, and his attitude. He had an *I don't give a damn* smirk on his face that made her want to slap him. Too bad they didn't do that kind of thing in their household.

"You owe your sister a new camera. I'd like a hundred dollars of your birthday money. Please get it for me now."

His lips compressed, but he dropped his feet from the footboard and shoved his way free of the chair. He went to the dresser and opened the top drawer. He sauntered over to her and held out the money. "I don't have a hundred, only sixty."

"Then I suggest you ask around about odd jobs in the neighborhood to earn the other forty, because you *will* pay for another camera. You may use our lawn mower, hedge trimmers, and weed eater, but you'll have to reimburse me for the gas."

"She freaking took my picture in a towel and nothing else."

"She deleted it before you destroyed the camera." She purposely opened the small compartment at the base of the device and removed the SD chip. Perhaps she could print the photos Jessica had taken. It wouldn't make up for her loss, but it might comfort her.

She placed the camera on the chest of drawers where Tad would see it every time he came into the room. "She's only eight, Tad. Was only being mischievous, not mean. She looks up to you so much."

"Then she shouldn't."

A dull ache settled at the base of her throat. "You may have gotten your wish because of your behavior today." She waited for him to reply. He remained silent, but looked away. "What if someone came into your room and took a hammer to your Xbox? How would you feel about that?"

His blue eyes, so much like hers, lit with resentment. "Don't pull your psychology bull-crap on me, Mom."

Disappointment lodged in the pit of her stomach. She tucked the SD chip into her pocket. "I was looking for a little empathy, and I was hoping you'd regret destroying something that meant a great deal to your sister. She's upset about the camera, but she's more upset that you were so cruel. And I've never known you to be purposely cruel before, Tad."

At his continued silence, she walked over and removed both controllers to the Xbox. "I think you need to stay in your room for a while and think some things through. When you've replaced your sister's camera, you can have your controllers back."

She closed the door behind her and stood outside for a moment. Everything remained ominously quiet. She ran her fingers through her short hair, still not used to the feel of it lying close to her head instead of swinging against her jaw. She put the controllers in her room in a shoebox and tucked them away on a shelf with several other boxes.

She walked back down the hall to Jessica's bedroom. Jess had curled on her side and turned her back to the room. Trish leaned back against the wall just outside the door. Tears of sympathy stung her eyes, but it was more than that. She was losing her son to hormones, teenage angst, and an anger she didn't understand.

Langley would be back in a while. He'd gone to the base to work on a schedule for the training he and his team were doing in a week or so.

They needed to talk about Tad. They needed to talk about a lot of things. She braced her hands on her knees and struggled against the draining welter of emotions.

They needed to find a way to connect again. They'd been able to do it before. They could do it again.

CHAPTER TWO

SAN DIEGO, 2016
SATURDAY, 6:30 a.m.

"**D**ERRICK ARMSTRONG WILL be out in six months." Hawk's tone was casual, and he continued filling out the requisition forms on his desk as though he was just shooting the shit while working.

It was Saturday and the office was quiet. Some personnel were off for the weekend, while others worked out in the field doing trainings. Langley couldn't be quite so casual. "How did you find out?"

Hawk glanced up, his gray eyes pale against his naturally bronze skin. "I know someone at the brig in Miramar. He's keeping me apprised."

"When he's released, he'll get a dismissal notice and be discharged?"

"Yeah. He pled guilty to unlawful imprisonment, terroristic threatening, assault, and the unlawful discharge of a firearm. He was lucky to get only five years."

Lucky. "He was the one, wasn't he?" Langley asked.

"He'll never admit it. But yeah. I believe he was. He and Brett were arguing before we arrived at the drop site. During the mission, Flash was on the roof of a building covering us. Greenback was covering our back door. Bowie and Doc got out before we knew anything was wrong, and neither of them had a beef with Cutter. And if Doc had wanted to kill him, he could easily have dragged his feet with medical care and just let him slip away. He worked hard to keep him going until we got him back to base. Derrick was the only one left besides me. And I was the first out of the building, and I know I didn't have anything to do with it."

"You wouldn't have gone back in for him if you'd been involved. You could have just let the timers run out while the rest of you bugged out."

"Doc swears he saw someone going back in through a window before I went in the front door. I believe it was Derrick. He was either having second thoughts and was going back in to help, or he wanted to finish him off before I found him."

Langley remained silent for a long moment. "So he gets off with five years after nearly killing a member of his team, damn near getting you blown to bits, and putting the rest in danger."

Hawk raised a dark brow. "He hasn't gotten off. He'll get that letter of dismissal before he's discharged from the brig. When he walks out of those doors, he'll have a very hard time finding work, he won't be able to own a firearm, and if he gets in trouble again as a civilian, they'll come down on him hard. He'll carry what he did with him for the rest of his life."

Langley nodded. Having it spelled out like that made it seem more like justice had been done. But he still had that queasy feeling in the pit of his stomach when he remembered the team returning from the mission. They'd all been…shell-shocked. All of their lives had been put in harm's way because of Derrick Armstrong's actions. For a time, they all pulled away from each other a little. Seeing Brett fighting for his life, and in a coma for more than a month, had shoved the idea of their own mortality in their faces. It was a tough time.

"We came back stronger after he went to jail," Langley commented.

"Yeah, we did. We lost Brett and Flash to other things, and now they're with other teams, but we've gained three good operators, and moved on as a team.

"And now we've lost Doc to his own team."

"And gained Logan and Sizemore. They've shaped up into really strong operators. And now, with Tyler taking Doc's place, the team's back in fighting form."

"Until you leave," Langley said. He was happy for Hawk's promotion to Lieutenant Commander. He was rising in the ranks just as he should. He was an exemplary officer, and had proven himself to be a top-notch operator and leader. He trained his men well, and was a natural-born leader. Every man in their team would follow him into hell and back if he asked it of them.

But, damn, it was going to be hard getting used to the team without him. And whoever they got to fill his shoes was going to have to have some big ones of their own to stand up to Hawk's reputation.

"Maybe you'll be going with me. You're up for promotion, and I'll still need an XO."

There were so few Master Chief promotions. Chances were he wouldn't make it.

"I'd like that, Hawk. But there's more than duty and work that goes into one of those promotions."

"I know. I'll be pulling for you. Captain Jackson will be too. It may come through."

He started to say something about Trish and held it back. If he could be Hawk's XO, and be responsible for the daily running and organization, he'd be out of the line of fire some of the time. That might ease some of Trish's worries.

Fifteen minutes later, Langley strode across the asphalt parking lot to his vehicle.

He'd finished the schedule while Hawk requisitioned the weapons they'd need for the training. But just when he thought he was finished, there was something else that needed to be done. Or was he stalling?

What he really needed to do was get things squared away with his wife. There was something going on with Trish, and he hadn't been able to get a handle on it. One minute she was great, and the next down his throat about some inconsequential nothing.

He got into the car and started the engine. The radio was on a rock station and he pushed the button to turn it off, enjoying the silence while he drove. It was the only time he had quiet in his life. He wove his way out of the parking lot to the main road, through the base to the gate, and out.

On the way home he pondered why the kids seemed just as edgy as he and Trish did. Tad had turned into a teenager while he was gone. A teenager with an attitude and a smart mouth.

Two years younger, Anna seemed to be very self-conscious and uncertain these days. Eight-year-old Jessica was the only one who hadn't changed while he was downrange. She'd been bitten by the photography bug, and ran around taking pictures of everything.

He wondered if she was chronicling the successes and failures in the adult relationships in their household. He and Trish were out of sync, and he couldn't pretend he didn't know why. Five deployments in the last five years... Thirteen battle deployments during their marriage.

He'd only been home with her and the kids a little more than two years out of every five. That meant he'd only been doing his job as a husband seven years out of the fifteen they'd been married.

If he could convince her to stick it out for another five, he could leave the teams with his full pension and move on to something different. Just five more years.

He could only remember her being this stressed once before. He'd deployed with his team while she was weak, alone, and struggling, and it had taken months for things between them to heal when he returned. He almost lost her then. He didn't want that to happen again.

But Uncle Sam signed his paycheck, and he didn't really have a choice.

After fifteen years of marriage, surely she wasn't ready to ring the bell. Not yet.

He just needed five more years, so he could go out with his pension. He'd work his ass off to ensure that happened. If she'd just hang in with him.

He'd never been this uncertain of her. Dealing with terrorists seemed a piece of cake compared to disappointing her. He dragged in a deep breath as he pulled into the drive and shut off the engine.

Anna rode her bicycle into the drive behind the car and passed it on the passenger side before she stopped to dismount. He shoved open the car door and got out.

"Hey, Annabelle." Her name was Annaliese, but he used his pet name to greet her. Her dark hair was a few shades lighter than his, but with her thick brows and lashes, she reminded him of his sister when small. Thank God her features were a little more symmetrical than his, and she'd been spared his long jaw. She'd hit a growth spurt while he was gone this time, and with her slender build, looked all arms and legs.

"Hey, Dad. Mom's been waiting for you to get home. Tad did something really bad, and he's in big trouble."

Shit. "I'd better go talk to your mom and see what's going on."

"You and I could hang out here by the pool and hope she doesn't find us."

"That bad, huh?"

Anna eyed him gravely and nodded.

Shit!

"We'll hang out by the pool after I go in and talk to Mom, okay?"

Anna nodded. "Okay." He was almost to the back door before she said, "Good luck."

That didn't sound good.

The house was silent. He wandered through the kitchen into the living room. The hall was dark, and all the bedroom doors were closed.

He stopped at Jessica's room and eased the door open. She lay curled on her bed, her dark hair mussed, and her eyes were red and swollen.

He bypassed Tad's door. He'd save the confrontation with his son for later. In the master bedroom, Trish had several piles of clothing on the floor. She must be cleaning out the closet.

He scanned the items and, seeing none of his stuff in the pile, breathed a sigh of relief. For a minute he thought she might be tossing *him* out.

"Anna said there was an issue this morning with Tad."

"He slammed Jessica's camera onto the floor as hard as he could and broke it. She took a picture of him after he got out of the shower wearing only a towel, and he was enraged."

She ran her fingers through her short cap of hair. He liked the new cut. It left her slender neck bare, and every time she turned her back, he wanted to press a kiss to that vulnerable, tender spot at her nape. "Jess cried herself to sleep. And he's not the least bit sorry."

"I'll go in and talk to him."

"I've never seen him like this, Langley. He's short-tempered, surly, and the way he broke the camera, it was violent." He read worry and hurt in her expression.

Langley reached for her, and she came into his arms. She laid her head against his shoulder like she was exhausted. "There's something going on with him, Langley."

He debated whether or not to pile more on, or just offer comfort. But if they didn't face what was going on between them…

"There's something going on with us, and he knows it. Talk to me, Trish."

She went completely still against him. "It won't do either of us any good to say the words out loud. Because there's nothing either of us can do or say to change things."

"Venting might help you."

"We'll just come right back to where we are, because there's no way of changing things. We're both locked into our paychecks, and we have to have the money."

Shocked, he was silent for a long moment. "You want to quit your job?"

"Yes, I do. They've doubled our caseloads, and I can barely breathe at work. The girls are good, but I can't give enough attention to Tad. He clearly resents me, and I don't understand why."

"It isn't you he resents, Trish. It's me. I just got back six weeks ago, and I'm already back to work. You're just an easier target because you're here and I'm not."

She leaned back to look up at him. "What do you plan to do about that?"

"The only thing I can. Talk to him." He'd never laid a hand on any of his kids but... "Unless you'd rather I spank his ass for breaking the camera."

Her eyes widened at the suggestion. "No. Of course not. I've already worked out a punishment. He has to work off the cost of another camera, and he can't have his X-box controls back until he does."

He pushed a little. "It isn't just the kids, is it?"

"No. It's—everything, Langley. I'm tired of dealing with everything alone." She flinched and closed her eyes. "I know that doesn't sound like a SEAL's good little wife, but Tad is wearing me down. Short of locking him in his room and sliding his food under the door, I don't know what else to do."

"I'll talk to him. See if I can't encourage an attitude adjustment."

"Thank you. I have to go to work." She pulled away and grabbed her purse.

This wedge between them refused to budge. "I love you, Trish. I know some of the guys I've been teamed with in the past weren't always faithful, but I've never strayed. You're the only woman I want. I don't want to lose you."

"I don't want us to lose each other, Langley. But I can't be three-quarters of a whole anymore."

Ouch, that hurt, more than a little.

"You have to find a way to pull your weight with your son. I can't do it alone anymore."

He followed her through the house to the front door while she collected her daily planner from the small office at the front of the house. She turned at the front door to look back at him.

"How long are you going to have to work weekends?" he asked.

"I don't know. I wish I could say this wasn't the new norm, but working five days a week just doesn't cut it. I have to do four home visits today, because it's the only time the parents are home for me to speak to them."

He nodded. "Be careful, Trish."

"I will." She picked up a sweater draped over the back of the couch and slipped it on.

He caught her arm when she started out the door. There had to be some physical contact between them. It was all he had right now. "I like the new haircut. It leaves that sweet spot right back here free." He brushed his fingertips down her neck. "I want to kiss you there every time I'm behind you." He bent his head and demonstrated, taking his time, and was rewarded when she shivered.

She turned to look over her shoulder at him, her pale blue eyes, scanning his face. "Talk to Tad and see if you can make some headway with him." She gripped his chin, rose on tiptoe and kissed him. "I may ask you do that again tonight."

He grinned and caught back a sigh of relief. At least she was still open to his sexual overtures. But then they'd always had a strong physical connection. *When he was home.* "I'm on it. I promise."

She nodded, opened the door, and strode down the front steps. Once behind the wheel, and noticing him still standing at the door watching her, she threw up a hand in a small wave.

He closed the door. It was time to deal with Tad. Right now. And if it took lighting up his son's behind, he'd do it. He wouldn't like it, but he'd do it.

CHAPTER THREE

SATURDAY, 12:00 p.m.

TRISH PULLED THE car over and parked. Almost done for the day. She looked forward to getting home to spend some time with the kids and Langley.

For a moment, she allowed herself to dwell on his soft kiss on the back of her neck, and the light in his eyes when she kissed him. They needed a few nights alone to iron out this tension between them. Maybe after making love a couple of times, or ten, she'd get her head on straight.

She turned her attention back to the job she was here to do, and studied the unkempt front yard, which was in dire need of mowing, especially around the sagging plastic pool with a shallow, scummy puddle of water. Then she reminded herself that just because a home looked neglected on the outside didn't necessarily mean there was an issue inside.

Mary Clarence did the right thing when she filed charges against her abusive husband a few days earlier. If Mary needed help with her yard, Tad could give it a quick mow that would last a couple of weeks. It would be good for him to give back, and learn the joy of helping someone less fortunate. Maybe if she kept carving away at the sullen almost-thirteen-year-old he was working on becoming, she'd break through that anger.

Trish climbed the one step to the plain concrete slab porch

with its narrow roof, and knocked on the bright red door, its color at odds with the rest of the house. She scanned the neglected yard once again while she waited for someone to answer.

The door's bright enthusiasm seemed at odds with the decidedly downtrodden feel to the place. The paint looked fresh. Had Mary Clarence felt a tiny bit of relief when her abusive husband was marched off the property and into a jail cell? There was a tiny spark of optimism to the color.

The lock on the door clicked as it was disengaged. Trish pasted a smile on her face and turned to face the person answering her knock.

A woman peeked out, her pale features all angles and hollows, a pointed chin, a thin blade of a nose, even her eye sockets seemed to protrude around her large brown eyes, as though she'd been without food for a while. Anxiety tightened her face as she remained partially hidden behind the door, a chain still looped from the doorjamb to the back side of the door, keeping the red barrier in place.

"Hello, Mrs. Clarence. My name is Trish Marks, and I'm your Child and Family Services caseworker. I'm here to do a home check, and to discuss your options for the services you and your children may qualify for."

"It isn't a good time, Ms. Marks. The children and I have been down with a stomach bug for the last two days. You don't want to catch this." She rested her forehead against the edge of the door, her face shining with a fine mist of sweat. "Can you come back tomorrow? We should be past the worst by then."

Trish caught movement in the crack between the door and the door jam. Was that a child...or someone else? "I can run down to the market and bring back some potato soup, crackers, and ginger ale for you."

"My next-door neighbor, Mrs. Franklin, has already done that." She flinched away from something behind the door. "Come back tomorrow."

The hairs on the back of Trish's neck stood up. "I will. Let me give you my card." She riffled through her purse and pulled out a business card with her office phone and cell on it. "If you or the children get any worse, call me, and I'll help you get transportation to the hospital."

Mary Clarence timidly reached for the card. "Thank you. I have to go." She shut the door.

Trish's heart hammered as she walked back down the sidewalk to her car. Who had been standing behind the door? Was it just her imagination, or was something going on here?

She turned to look back at the house and tugged her cell phone from the front pocket of her organizer. She slid her thumb over the surface of her phone and scrolled down and punched the number for the sheriff's department. She asked for one of the deputies she worked with frequently.

"Marshall, can you tell me if Thomas Clarence has been released?"

"I'll look it up for you." The sound of keys being tapped came across the line. "He was released this morning."

"Dear God. He wasn't supposed to be released. He's threatened to kill his wife, beat her to a pulp, and she has an EPO out against him. I think he's here at the house. I think he was behind the door threatening his wife while I was speaking to her."

"Are you still at the house?"

"Yes."

"Call her. See if you can get her to pick up. Call me back."

Trish slid into the front seat and closed the door. She shuffled through Mary Clarence's file, found the number, and punched it in.

The phone rang and was on its way to six times before it was picked up. "Hello." A breathless female voice answered.

"Mrs. Clarence?"

"Yes."

"This is Trish Marks again. Are you alone?"

"No, I'm not."

"Is your husband there?"

Her only answer was unsteady breathing.

"Are you and the girls in danger?"

"Yes."

"Is he armed?"

"Yes."

Her mouth went dry and her heart drummed in her ears. "Tell him I just called to verify I have your number down correctly. I've already called the police. Can you get the girls and close them up in a bedroom?"

"I will."

"I'm going to do all I can to help you, Mary."

"Thank you."

"The police are waiting for my call."

Her voice dropped to a whisper. "Hurry."

"I will."

Trish's fingers rushed to end the call and reconnect to Marshall. "You have to get someone here now. He's there. She says he's armed, and they're in danger. I told her to try and get the kids into a bedroom away from him."

"I'm on it. Don't go near the house."

"I won't. For God's sake, don't let them arrive here with sirens wailing."

"Pull around the corner, and I'll meet you there. I have done this before, Trish."

"Do it faster," she urged and hung up.

She couldn't just leave. She had to stay. She had information on the Clarence family the police might be able to use.

She started the car and pulled around the corner, parking where she could still see the Clarence house. She called her office and punched in the number for one of the other social workers. "Irene, I've had to call the police. They released Thomas Clarence without notifying us or his wife. He's inside the house, and he's armed. It may be a hostage situation, and I'm waiting for the police to show up now. Can you change my last two appointments, and space them out over the next few days?"

"Sweet Jesus! I'm on it. Stay out of the line of fire."

"I am. I've pulled around the corner out of the way. I thought they might need background on the case and him when they arrive."

"That's a good idea. I'll make those calls. Be safe."

"Thanks." She'd done some background on both Mary Clarence and her abusive husband, Thomas, when the case first hit her desk three days before. She scanned the information now for anything that might be helpful.

At a tap on the driver's window she jumped and looked up. The hole at the end of the pistol's barrel looked as big as a cannon pressed against the driver's side window. The square-jawed face behind the weapon was only familiar because of the pictures she'd just been looking at.

Trish's breath caught inside her chest, and she couldn't release the air from her lungs. Her stomach curdled, and every instinct in her screamed, *get away from the gun!*

She'd fired Langley's service weapon a time or two, but had never been a fan of firearms, and he was careful to keep his Sig at the base, or secured in a lockbox on a shelf in the closet. Only he had the key to it.

"Get outta the car, bitch." The man's voice was muffled through the glass. He jerked at the door, but it was locked. "I will shoot you through the glass. Open the fuckin' door."

She felt nauseous as she hit the button to unlock the door.

Thomas Clarence jerked it open and grabbed her arm to drag her out of the seat. He caught her back against him with an arm across her shoulders, and pressed the gun to her temple hard enough to hurt.

"Take the car. The keys are in the ignition."

"What are you doin' sitting here?"

"I just left someone's house and was looking up my next appointment. I needed to program my GPS in order to find the house." She pointed to the GPS navigation device mounted on the windshield. "Please don't hurt me."

"Do you know who I am?"

"No."

"You're trying to take my family away from me."

"I don't understand."

"You're from family services, ain't you?"

"Yes."

He stuck the gun beneath her chin. Her heart seemed to stop, and her body froze. He was out of control. She was going to die if she couldn't talk him out of the rage coming to a boil inside him.

She couldn't even talk her twelve-year-old son out of his anger. How was she supposed to deal with an enraged husband?

Her breathing came in shallow gasps, and her entire body shook. "My job is to try and get medical services for the family, and make sure they get enough support to keep a roof over their heads and food on the table. Why would you think that I'm trying to take your family away from you, if all I'm trying to do is help them survive?"

"You're interfering with my family, bitch. We don't need no handouts."

"If you're Mr. Clarence, your family isn't signed up for any help. Not yet."

"You think you're real smart, don't you? The same as those fucking cops who hauled me off to jail the other night. Well, I ain't goin' back to jail, and Mary and my kids ain't goin' on without me, neither."

Did he mean he was going to kill them and himself? "Why would you want to hurt the people you love, Mr. Clarence?"

The gun drifted away from beneath her chin, and Trish drew a slow, shallow breath.

"She's not gettin' rid of me. She's my wife, and those kids are *mine*. They belong to me."

Trish eased a hand up toward the gun. If only she could grab the barrel and hold it away from her. "You can go to family counseling, Mr. Clarence, to help settle your differences with your wife. You can still be a family."

"Not with you showing her how she can go on without me."

The familiar black and white Charger the county sheriffs drove came around the corner and started up the street. When the gun barrel swung back toward her, Trish caught it and held it away from her face. "I have a family of my own, and I'm not going to let you shoot me."

"Try and stop me, bitch." Clarence jerked at the gun, but Trish held on while she let her legs relax beneath her, forcing him to bend and hold her weight. Then she bit into his wrist and held on. Clarence yelled and released his grip on her as he tried to wrench his hand free. If he got loose, he'd shoot her. He punched her on the back of the head with his fist, and pain ricocheted through her neck.

The front grill of the black and white jumped the curb and hit the sidewalk right in front of them. Truman Marshall's six-foot-four frame leaped out of the car with his weapon in hand.

"Get the hell away from her," he shouted. "Drop the weapon."

Clarence heaved back and kneed Trish in the ribs just beneath her breast, nearly lifting her off the ground. Air exploded from her lungs, and she lost her grip on his hand and sprawled back on the sidewalk, hitting her head so hard she saw white, then black. Clarence raised the gun and pointed it toward Marshall, then let out a bellow of rage and fired.

The bark of Marshall's service weapon seemed to echo as he fired. Clarence tumbled back, the twenty-two pistol gripped in his hand going off again as he fell. He twisted around and ran back toward the houses.

Marshall ran from behind his vehicle and gave chase.

When her ears stopped ringing, Trish became aware of the distant sound of traffic two blocks over. The sensation of not being able to catch her breath started to overwhelm her.

Great. She was having a panic attack after everything was over. She tried to roll to her feet, but found her body wouldn't respond. There was something wrong.

The sound of running feet approached. Marshall's huge shoulders and round head popped into her range of vision. "Trish?" The first time he said her name it was like an inquiry. "Trish—" His panicked shout caused her to jerk.

A horrible pain built in her chest, arrowing deeper by the moment.

"Just lie still." The deputy's hand seemed the size of a baseball mitt as he pressed down against her ribcage. He keyed his radio, identifying himself and giving his location. "I have shots fired. The suspect is still at large. I need a supervisor. I have a victim down. She has a gunshot wound to the right chest, and she's bleeding heavily. I need an ambulance *now!*"

Every breath felt like she was trying to breathe underwater. She'd been shot. It didn't seem possible. The son-of-a-bitch actually shot her. She felt cold and nausea rolling her stomach into a tight ball, and she fought the need to throw up. She reached out to grip Marshall's wrist, but her arm couldn't seem to work quite right. He snatched the waving limb in midair and gripped it hard.

She thought of Langley. She wouldn't leave him with that burden of guilt any more than he would her. "Langley." Her voice sounded like a puff of air. "Love him."

"Don't you go there, Trish," Marshall yelled, as if the strength of his voice would keep her from giving into the blackness creeping around the edges of her vision.

Sirens warbled in the distance, getting closer. "Just hold on. They're coming."

She'd never realized how noble Marshall's African-American features looked, or how intense a brown his eyes were. She remembered the child custody case where they met. He'd been sympathetic but professional, and defused the situation by taking the father outside and talking to him while the children got their clothing together. The man was weeping openly, but hadn't been violent as so many were.

Marshall did his job, she did hers, and months would go by when she didn't have to access him as a contact. She didn't even know if he was married or had children. But he was holding her hand and talking to her now, urging her to keep breathing.

Two different sirens converged on the street. Trish's vision narrowed to a tunnel. She didn't want to leave her children. They needed her.

She felt so tired. Pushing air in and out took more and more effort. There was a boulder sitting on her chest, and she couldn't get enough air. She coughed and pushed against Marshall's hand so she could roll on her side. He seemed to sense what she needed and eased her over.

Her vision went from gray to black. She closed her eyes and surrendered.

CHAPTER FOUR

SATURDAY, 1:00 p.m.

L ANGLEY STUDIED HIS son's sullen expression. Tad had been asleep when he attempted this talk the first time.

Now he was awake, Tad was giving him a solid dose of what Trish described earlier today. His body language screamed *I don't give a shit*, but his ears remained bright red with temper.

Langley took a step farther into the room so Tad had to tilt his head back to look up at him. Sometimes it helped to put a little dominant body language into the equation. Jesus, he was using psychology on his twelve-year-old to gain the upper hand.

"You realize you've hurt your sister in a way she'll never forget. She'll forgive you, eventually, but she won't forget what you did today."

"Good. Maybe she'll stay out of my room."

"I'm sure she will. I expect you to stay out of hers from now on, too."

"No problem."

At his snappy answer, Langley clenched his hands into fists. "Your mother's already taken your X-box. Keep up with the attitude, and you'll be staring at these four walls for the next week without a television as well."

Tad's head jerked up and his blue eyes, so much like Trish's, glinted with a combination of resentment and fear before he looked away.

"Are you going to tell me what's going on, or are you going to continue digging a hole for yourself with your mouth?"

Silence stretched, filling the room. Langley leaned against the chest of drawers and prepared to wait until Tad broke it.

"You and Mom don't like each other anymore."

"We love each other, Tad."

"You don't act like it."

He gripped his thin legs, and Langley saw himself in the gesture.

Tad's voice dropped. "Or at least Mom doesn't."

Langley thought about the final moment they had before Trish left for work. He'd done a lot of thinking before he walked into this room, and what he'd figured out didn't make him happy.

Trish was overwhelmed right now, and she needed more help than he could give her. He'd dropped the ball again, and his job made it difficult for him to pick it back up.

But how could he explain the ups and downs of a marriage to a twelve-year-old?

"Tad, your mom and I have been married fifteen years, and she's had to do everything alone more than half the time we've been married, because I've been gone. She's had to carry the weight of *everything* without me.

"Her job's gotten really hard the last couple of months, because they've doubled her caseload, and she's having to work weekends and longer hours to keep up. She's tired when she gets home. But she still has the same responsibility for taking care of you and your sisters, the house, and the bills."

"You help," Tad broke in.

Langley smiled half-heartedly at his son's defense of him. "When I'm here, but I'm not always here. I'm home for stretches of time, but in between…she has to be Mom and Dad to you and your sisters. You know that, and I know it. I had to leave this morning. Who fixed your breakfast and loaded the dishwasher while I was gone?"

"Mom."

"Who folded your laundry and put it in the basket for you to put away?"

"Mom."

"Who dealt with your meltdown and the consequences before she had to leave for work?"

Tad's head dropped, as did his voice. "Mom."

"She's working sixty-hour weeks, Tad. How many hours a day is that in a six-day week?"

"Ten."

"But she still picked up the drinks for your team on Thursday, made sure your uniform was clean, and came to the game, didn't she?"

"Yeah."

"She does those things because she knows they're important to you, because you're important to her. She does things for all of us, including me, because she loves us."

Relief and regret hit him as tears ran down Tad's cheeks. It was hard to stand there and watch his son cry without offering him support or sympathy. He waited several moments to allow the reality of how upset he was with his son to sink in before he moved to sit down on the end of the bed. "I need your help, Tad."

Using the hem of his T-shirt, Tad dried his face. "With what?"

"I need you to help me figure out how we can help Mom not have so much to do around here, so she can spend more time with us."

Tad attempted to look pitiful and almost succeeded. "Mom said I have to ask around the neighborhood for yard work jobs to earn enough money to pay for another camera for Jessica."

"You broke it. It's your responsibility to replace it."

Tad's head dropped again.

"I thought it might be a good idea to revamp the household chore schedule and add a few things that you and your sisters can do to help out more when I'm not here. Like take out the trash, clean the bathroom, load the dishwasher, and fold the laundry."

"Okay."

"And it wouldn't hurt to apologize to your sister, too."

Tad shot him a resentful look, and Langley gritted his teeth and fought the urge to shake the shit out of him. He was getting a full dose of what Trish had been dealing with for months. If she could be patient, so could he, but damn it was hard. "Think about it."

He left the bedroom much more optimistic than when he entered it. He made some real headway with Tad, he was certain of it. He paused outside Jessica's door. She'd been asleep for a while, but now sat on the side of her bed.

Jess was their most sensitive child. A true blend of the two of them, with her mother's blue eyes, and his dark hair and brows, she was the one he was going to worry about when she started dating. Both his girls were beautiful, but Jessica was going to be gorgeous, and have that special inner beauty that would draw guys right in. It was guaranteed to drive him crazy trying to protect her.

He wandered into the room, sat down on the bed, and wrapped an arm around her. She leaned into him and cuddled close. He pressed a kiss to the top of her head. "Mom and I have both spoken to Tad. He's lost his X-box privileges, and he has to earn the money to replace the camera. He owes you an apology, too."

He was surprised when she didn't cry. It worried him more when she just curled in closer and remained silent. "It's going to be okay, Jess."

She nodded. "Why are boys so mean?"

"Tad isn't always mean. He's good to you and Anna most of the time."

"Ethan Morgan and Bobby Alexander are mean to me at school."

Shit! What next? "Just you? Or everyone?"

"Just me and Sarah Donner."

He wracked his brain to identify Sarah Donner. "Is that the little girl with blond hair down to her waist?"

"Yes."

"Boys sometimes do things to get your attention because they like you."

Jessica looked up at him. "Being mean to me isn't going to make me like either of them."

He bit the inside of his lip to keep from smiling. "You are very smart. Have I told you that lately?"

She smiled for the first time. "You tell me that all the time."

"If they keep picking on you, tell your teacher. And if that doesn't work, tell them you're going to tell your dad, and he'll have a nice visit with theirs."

She snuggled up to him and gave him a squeeze as far as her arms could reach.

Only your kids could make you feel ten feet tall or as helpless as hell. "Anna and I are going to hang out together. Why don't you join us, and we'll watch a movie together? Or we can hang out by the pool. We can play some volleyball."

"I'd rather watch a movie."

"Okay. I'll go round up your sister."

Anna was still riding her bicycle up and down the sidewalk in front of the house. He called her in, and they settled in the family room. He'd sit through anything the girls picked, but he hoped it wasn't going to be a cartoon. Luckily, they picked an action/adventure.

With a daughter on each side, he kicked off his shoes and propped his bare feet on the coffee table.

The opening credits had just begun when the doorbell sounded.

"I'll get it," Anna said and ran down the hall to the front of the house. She returned almost immediately, her expression so anxious he was already getting to his feet before she spoke. "Dad, the police are at the door."

Adrenaline hit his system, and his heart raced. Langley tried to keep his expression neutral. "Stay here and watch the movie. I'll go see what they need."

Once out of the family room he rushed to get to the front door. One patrol officer stood on the front stoop, the other out in the yard. They both looked very young, and both looked like they wished they were anywhere but here.

"Mr. Marks?"

"Yes."

"Sir, there's been an incident concerning your wife. She's at the hospital."

Police officers didn't come to the house to tell you about a fender-bender or some other minor thing. "What's happened?"

"Sir. She's been shot."

The words punched a hole right through him. He gripped the door facing to stay on his feet. "Shot? *Shot?*" He had to go to her. "What hospital has she been taken to?"

"She's at Balboa, sir. We'll take you there."

It must be bad if they had come to get him. He whipped his phone out of his pocket, scrolled, then hit Hawk's number. He couldn't seem to get his breath. "I need you to come to the house and stay with my kids. Trish has been shot."

CHAPTER FIVE

SATURDAY, 6:00 p.m.

LIGHT PIERCED TRISH'S eyelids, drawing her toward consciousness. She fought against it and the rising pain in her chest. She tried to swallow and couldn't. Something was in her mouth, blocking her throat. She reached for the obstacle, but was so weak she couldn't fight the pressure of other hands as they redirected hers.

"Trish?" Langley's voice drew her closer to the surface. She didn't want to go there yet.

What if he told her something horrible had happened? She couldn't bear to hear it right now.

Exhaustion weighted her limbs.

Was that a baby crying?

She drifted back to sleep.

JUNE 28, 2008

IT HAD BEEN a good day. A relaxing day.

In the shade of the house, with a breeze cooling them, it was even comfortable.

The baby had barely cried, and Langley, God bless him, took

Tad and Anna to the beach to play for a couple of hours.

She looked down the street, expecting to see the car at any moment. She hoped she was over the hump of recovery after Jessica's birth. It had been difficult, and the stress of breast-feeding, plus the loss of so much blood, drained her.

She still didn't feel herself. She felt shaky, weak, and exhausted. Just walking across the floor took far more effort than usual.

If only her mother hadn't needed to return to Kansas. She'd been such help the two weeks she was here, and Trish had really needed her, since Langley was away on a training.

But her mother had a life too, her job, her house. She'd enjoyed the children. Undoubtedly she loved them. But she'd begun to wilt around the edges before leaving. Tad was only four, Anna two, and now a newborn. Her mother, though just this side of fifty, had been glad to go home to her quiet house and her friends.

Jessica lay under an awning attached to her small playpen, her short legs tucked under her belly and her butt in the air. She weighed eight pounds two ounces at birth, but was already growing. She was a good baby during the day, but wasn't sleeping at night. Not unexpected. They were all sleep-deprived.

Trish caught a glimpse through the neighbor's yard of their red Malibu as it turned the corner. Langley pulled into the driveway, got out of the car, and walked around to release Tad from his car seat first.

Tad ran over to give her a hug, his cheeks sun-kissed and sand glittering on his skin. "We missed you, Mommy."

"I missed you, too. Why don't you go around and get the water hose and let Daddy spray you off a little before you go in the house?"

"I can do it myself." He might look like her, but his personality was all Langley, and she encouraged his independence in every way she could.

He couldn't make much mess outside in the grass spraying himself down, and she could strip his clothes off before he went inside. "Why don't you give it a try, and if there's any extra sand left, Daddy will take care of it."

He dashed back down the wooden stairs to the deck and around the side of the house to the water hose.

Langley climbed the steps with Anna in his arms. His skin was tanned from being out in the desert sun the past week, and his grayish-green eyes, the same color as Anna's, looked pale. His beard-darkened jaw, so strong and masculine, drew her attention. Even after nearly eight years of marriage, her heart still leaped when she saw him, even after brief separations.

Anna's dark head rested on his shoulder, and she cuddled against his broad chest, limp and soundly asleep. Seeing him hold one of their children, his care and tenderness toward them, never failed to move her.

He brushed his chin against Anna's hair. "She's worn herself out on the beach building a sand castle with Tad. I'll put her down."

Trish unlatched Anna's sandy shoes, dusted her tiny feet, and set the shoes on the table. "Thanks, Langley."

He carried their daughter inside.

Tad ran around the side of the house, soaking wet, his pale blond hair sticking up on top of his head like spikes. Trish laughed and tugged him between her legs. She stripped him, bundled his sopping clothing onto the table next to her, and grabbed a beach towel from the railing of the deck to dry him off.

"Go into your room and put on dry underwear and your Spiderman sweatpants. Daddy's in there, so he can help you if you need it. You can take a bath in a little while."

He used his favorite phrase, "I can do it myself," before he took off running toward the back door. His narrow, bare behind, a hand's-width across, glowed white compared to the light tan darkening his back and lower legs. He was going to be lean and tall like his father. She could already see the similarities in his bone structure.

She hung his discarded clothes across the deck railing to dry.

Langley slipped out the door ten minutes later. "He's sitting in front of the television watching a Spiderman cartoon in his Spidey pants, and I suspect he'll probably crash soon. I took them to a taco place. You know the one that has the bite-sized tacos? Anna loved them.

"In fact, I brought you some. No sauce, so it won't bother the baby." He went back out to the car, brought in a bag, and set it on the table next to her.

He paused a moment. "We got you something at the beach today."

"What is it?"

He drew a small bouquet of cornhusk roses from behind his back, each flower tipped along its edges very lightly with color. "A girl was making these on the beach. Tad said the blue one was from him and Anna picked the peach one. I chose a yellow one for Jessica, and a red one from me."

Tears pricked Trish's eyes as she took them. "They're beautiful. Thank you, Langley."

"You're welcome, sweetheart." He leaned down and brushed her lips with his own.

She looped an arm around his neck and rested her head on his shoulder. He knelt to nestle between her legs and hold her.

"What is it?"

"I can't seem to get my feet under me this time, Langley."

"You had a bad time of it, honey. The doc said you'd have to take things slow for a while."

She nodded against his shoulder and breathed in the briny scent of the sea, laundry soap, and Langley, while she fought against the pain. She knew her husband. Knew his tells. He was taking the kids, spending one-on-one time with them. Going out of his way to be useful. Not that he didn't do that a lot when he was here, but he'd been particularly attentive the last few days.

"I think we all need a nap," he suggested.

She nodded again. He stood and backed away, holding his hand out to help her push up from the chair.

"I'll get the baby. You go ahead and lie down for a while."

She gathered the roses and held them against her chest. "When do you leave?"

His features blanked in surprise, but his green gaze remained focused on the baby. "Tomorrow."

The shock of it struck her silent. She wished him already gone. Dealing with his leaving was harder than his absence.

And she couldn't say a damn thing. It was against the military wife code to say anything, in case something happened to him while he was gone. She didn't want to live with that guilt. Didn't want him carrying it into battle.

She already knew what he was when she married him. She watched him fly away during their engagement, after their wedding, during all three pregnancies.

She needed him now. She wasn't steady. She needed to be steadier before he left again.

But she turned and walked into the house, because there wasn't anything else to say.

She placed the roses on the dresser. In the mirror, she looked pale, washed-out, and exhausted. Almost too tired to block off the self-pitying feelings of abandonment that rose up to slash at her.

She lay down on the bed and curled on her side, her back to the door.

Langley came in a few minutes later and lay behind her to spoon, his long legs curled beneath hers. "Everyone's asleep. We'd better grab some shut-eye while we can."

"Jessica will be our last baby," she announced.

"If that's what you want, Trish. I'm happy with three."

"That's what I want."

"Physically you've experienced a trauma. Wait until you're back from it before you make a firm decision."

No. She needed to face up to it now. Financially, they couldn't afford any more. And with Langley always gone, she couldn't handle any more alone. Tears rose up like a fist at the back of her throat. Exhaustion curled around her tighter than Langley's arms.

"I love you, Trish."

She knew he did, but she needed him to just this once put her first. But she couldn't demand something he was unable give. The choice was out of his hands. But it didn't ease the hurt. The silence stretched on until she said, "I love you too, Langley."

CHAPTER SIX

SATURDAY, 7:00 p.m.

LANGLEY CLENCHED AND unclenched his hands in frustration. The medical personnel kept coming in and checking on her, but they didn't want her to wake up just yet.

After that one attempt to grab the trach tube, they gave her sedation and she settled back into unconsciousness. They said it was easier for her to tolerate the trach if she remained sedated.

Her short, pale blond hair was stuck to her head from the hat they covered it with during surgery. Her redhead complexion was so pale, every freckle stood out across her nose, and even the veins beneath the skin in her temples and neck were visible.

It wasn't supposed to be her flat on her back with tubes coming out of her. After all the dangerous situations he made it through without a scratch, what kind of cosmic joke was this that she was the one who'd been shot?

If the deputy, Truman Marshall, hadn't stayed with her and gotten her medical attention so quickly...

And the sorry son of a bitch who shot her was still at large, though they were certain he was wounded. There was a blood trail at the scene, but the man had disappeared.

As far as Langley was concerned, Marshall had done the world and Clarence's wife a favor by shooting him. The deputy deserved a medal. And he hoped Clarence was suffering from his wound.

He deserved it.

Langley ran a hand over his face. Anger could only sustain him for so long. After six hours in the hospital, he was running out of patience, and his concern was escalating fast.

Where the hell was the fucker? They needed to find him and lock him up. What if he decided to show up here?

He studied the fragile line of Trish's jaw, the bluish hollows beneath her eyes, the fan of her lashes. When he cupped her oval face in his hands and kissed her it felt…perfect. Even after fifteen years of marriage, he still felt that rush of need whenever she was near. Well…when the kids weren't interrupting.

Why couldn't he figure out what was going on with her right now? They had always been so in tune with each other.

All except that time after Jess was born. They'd taken a trip to wine country for some time alone after he got back from the deployment that had dragged him away from her then. He remembered it so vividly, because he really thought she'd been on the verge of giving him his walking papers. But she hadn't.

But their life together changed after that, and it led them to this moment, led her to where she was right now.

MARCH 9, 2009

LANGLEY WOUND HIS way down the two-lane road. The fields were lush and verdant with rows of grapevines and clumps of trees.

"I think it's this next turn."

He swung the steering wheel to the right and followed the shady road. After a quarter of a mile, the inn came into sight. Built of light brown stone, it sprawled across an emerald green lawn, and looked like a Swiss chalet. The windows glittered in the afternoon sun.

"It looks lovely, Langley," Trish breathed.

He grinned as he took in Trish's windblown blond hair and sun-flushed cheeks. The sprinkle of freckles that marched across the bridge of her nose only added to the country girl prettiness his wife rocked. She had lost her post-baby weight and more, though. She was thinner than he liked to see her. But he was hesitant about saying anything. Didn't think it would be welcome.

He'd been home five days, and there was still a distance between them he couldn't seem to breach. She'd been at work every day, and kids' stuff had pretty much taken over the rest of her time and attention. And she dropped into bed like a zombie by the time she got everything done. As for making love, she'd shown zero interest. Which had never happened before.

He attempted to keep some levity in his tone. "They give you as much wine as you can drink while you're here, so if you feel the need to tie one on, the kids aren't here, and I'll take good care of you."

She quirked an eyebrow at him. "I'm not sure I even like wine. And I didn't think you did at all."

"Maybe I'll learn to like it. Maybe I just haven't tasted the right kind."

He pulled up in front of the chalet, found an empty space in the lot, and parked.

"Why did you choose to bring me here, Langley?" Trish's pale blue eyes searched his face.

"Because I thought you'd enjoy something more girly than a Padre's game and a beer, and I want us to have some time for just the two of us. They have a spa here, and you can have a massage, facial, and whatever other stuff they offer."

Besides when his wife was happy, she always returned the favor and made him happy. It had been nine months since he made love with his wife. He'd rubbed her back, hugged her, and kissed her, but with her on bed rest at the end of the pregnancy, they hadn't made love in nearly ten. He was feeling the strain.

She didn't smile when she said, "And you're hoping to get laid?"

"That might have played a small"—he held up a hand with his thumb and forefinger apart an inch—"part in it. We do seem to have little people running around interrupting the mood on a constant basis." *And you've seemed a little exhausted,* he added to himself.

Trish tilted her head back against the headrest.

"We need some time together without the kids, Trish. We need to work on us."

A wry grimace tilted her mouth. "I love them. I can't believe how much I love them. But two minutes in a room without someone calling my name would be wonderful."

"Then why are you feeling guilty about being here?" Langley asked. "It's just a weekend. Two days out of years and years of being their mother."

There was no twinkle in her eye when she leveled her gaze at his face. "It's a Mom thing. It's ingrained into our DNA."

He thought about that a moment. Did she think it was just moms?

Didn't she know how guilty he felt every time he had to board a plane and fly away from them? How it hurt to miss seeing each one of them taking their first step, or doing all the other things they did to grow and become their own person? How it tore his heart out to be a stranger to his children when he returned home, and they had to relearn how to connect with him each time?

Seven-month old Jess was wary of him this time. Hadn't wanted to come to him. He understood, but it had broken his heart right there on the tarmac.

All that aside, the thing was...he needed Trish, too. Probably more than she needed him. Way more.

To keep from voicing all that, he unbuckled his seat belt and got out of the car. He went around the trunk to get the suitcases. Trish joined him there and reached for her own. "What were you going to say?"

Langley looked up. "We can talk about it later. I'm ready for a beer, if they'll give me one, and a few minutes alone with my wife."

He smiled at the soft color that touched Trish's cheeks. "Nearly ten years of marriage, and I can still make you blush."

Her expression remained neutral.

All right, he'd known they had some work to do here. But he had hoped.... He hefted their bags out of the car and carted them across the parking area to the sidewalk and into the hotel. He handed Trish the credit card and let her check them in.

The interior of the hotel was all golden, warm wood and bold colors. Red area rugs were scattered around the tile floor. A large fireplace. Water and coffee were set out in the lobby, with a plate of pastries and cookies under a glass dome.

"We'll send a bottle of wine up to your room in just a few moments," the woman behind the counter said as she handed Trish the credit card. "Would you prefer red or white?"

Langley shrugged as Trish looked back over her shoulder at him. What did a beer guy know about wine?

"White, please," Trish said.

"The dining room is open for breakfast between six-thirty and ten. Lunch is served from eleven until four, and dinner from five until nine. We do a tasting every afternoon at four, with cheese and crackers served then. If you need anything at all, don't hesitate to call the front desk."

"Thank you." Trish slipped the key into a small pocket on her sundress.

They headed around the corner from the front desk to the elevator and rode up to the second floor. Trish unlocked the door and held it wide for him as he carried their luggage into the room.

He'd booked a suite so they could have a little more space. He didn't want her to feel crowded like she was at home. The furnishings were a light oak that reflected the warm woodwork and tiled floors, again covered by thick area rugs.

Brightly-colored abstract artwork hung on the walls. A desk and a cabinet housing a small refrigerator, microwave and television stretched along one wall. A couch, coffee table, and a chair faced them. Through a door he could see the bed and a nightstand.

Trish went to the far end to open the sliding glass door and wander out onto the balcony.

Langley dumped the luggage at the foot of the bed and sauntered out to join her. A large, kidney-shaped pool glittered pale blue below them, with shrubs and flowers camouflaging the chain link fence bordering it. Beyond the fence, row after row of grapevines marched across the valley and up the nearby hills. It was a beautiful place, picturesque. The sun touched his skin like a warm hand, and he tilted his head back and allowed it to bathe his face.

"I'd think you'd have had enough sun in Iraq, Camp Billy Machen, and all the other hot, dry places you've been," Trish commented.

"It's gentler here. More like a caress than a slap." She didn't bitch or lose her temper, she just made those flat comments, like a stranger who knew you a little, but not well enough to care. Had her love for him died? A wave of pain hit him, his heart thundered against his ribs, and he reached out blindly and gripped the balcony railing.

If there wasn't a chance they could get past this, he needed to know now and save himself the heartache. "Do you think you'll ever forgive me for leaving you this deployment, Trish?"

She remained silent for a long moment. "We have three children together, Langley. The youngest seven months old. If we break up, you'll move on with your life, and so will we, but the children will lose their home, and their father. They'll see you even less than they do already. All the things we hoped and dreamed for them will be gone. We're both used to making sacrifices, and they're more important than either of us."

If he'd been punched in the chest by a rifle stock, it couldn't have hurt as much. "So the only reason you'll be staying with me is for the children?"

A small crack showed in her composure and her eyes grew shiny with tears. "No. I couldn't do that. But I'm so angry with you right now..." She swallowed. "The only thing I'm certain of is they have to come first."

"You know I didn't want to leave you and the children, Trish. You have to know that it tears me apart every time I have to leave. It nearly killed me to go, knowing you needed me."

She stared at him. "You never said anything. You just got your gear and left."

His eyes burnt. "I'm telling you now. If I'd said it before…it would have made it harder for me to leave. To do what I had to do."

She stared off into the distance, silent.

"This is who I am. This is what I do."

He knew he'd said the wrong thing when she turned and walked back into their room.

Langley ran a hand over his face. She had a right to be upset.

She wouldn't be on his ass if she didn't still love him.

But she wasn't on his ass.

She was cool, distant, not arguing with him. She'd held on to this for seven months. Seven months of stewing and pain. That scared the hell out of him.

Trish didn't give up any easier than he did. They had nine years together. Eleven, if you counted the two years they lived together before they married. He had to believe she would want to hold their marriage together.

When he heard a knock, he turned to join her in the room.

One of the bellmen stood at the door with a bottle of wine and a corkscrew. After he left, Trish twisted the device into the cork. "I'm going to open it now. I think I could use a drink."

She drank sparingly at home, always mindful of the kids. He drank beer if he was mowing the grass on a hot day, or entertaining his teammates, but for the most part they drank iced tea or water. One glass of wine and she'd be ready to nod off for a nap.

Maybe that was exactly what they needed.

An ice bucket and an assortment of glasses sat on a tray beside the television. Langley retrieved two wine glasses and held them, waiting for her to pour. She filled them midway and set the small bottle on the tray.

She raised the glass to her lips and took a sip. "It isn't bad. I might learn to like it."

Langley took a drink and controlled the grimace. "Maybe I need to do some research and learn about wines. The brochure for this place said they've won awards for theirs."

Trish stretched out on the bed and kicked off her shoes. The sundress she wore clung to her slender shape and emphasized how thin she was now.

Maybe there was something more going on. Maybe she was sick. Worry gave him a punch to the gut. He looked down at the wine in his glass and swirled it.

"They're having a tasting in…" She glanced at her wrist. "An hour. You can try out several and find one you like."

"Maybe. You plan to go, don't you?" At this point he wasn't sure she wanted to be in the same room with him.

"Yes. You said they dress for dinner."

"Yeah. I brought dress pants and a sports coat. I'm hoping not to have to wear a tie."

"You can stick it in your pocket just in case, and put it on if they insist."

"You'd tell me if there was something wrong with you, wouldn't you Trish?"

She looked up surprised. "Why would you think there's something wrong. Langley?"

"You're thinner than you usually are."

She took a sip of wine and held it in her mouth for a moment before swallowing. "I have three children under the age of five, one of whom learned to sleep through the night just two weeks ago, and I work fifty hours a week. By the time I get around to eating, I'm too tired to care about food. I'm more interested in sleeping."

Ask a stupid question. "I'll be home for the next three weeks. You can sleep as much as you want."

"Do you plan on being Mr. Mom for the next three weeks?" she asked. "I don't have any vacation or sick days left to stay home with you and the children."

"I can handle them. Besides, it will give me a chance to connect with Tad and Anna again, and win Jessica over."

For the first time he saw compassion in her expression. "She hasn't been around many men since you've been gone. My dad came out for a few days, and your brother Jason came out for a week with Karen. They're the only two men who've hung out at the house. She's only seen you on a computer screen. You're bigger in person, and your voice is deep."

"How'd she do with your dad and Jason?"

"It took her a while, but she eventually let them hold her. But she'd eye them like they were some kind of alien life form she was trying to figure out."

"Sort of like she does with me." He'd tried not to let it get to him that she didn't want him getting close, but it did. She was his daughter, and he loved her. "If I'm there alone with all three of them, she'll get used to me."

She finished her wine and set the glass on the nightstand. "Be my guest, Mr. Mom. If it gets to be too much for you, I'll still have to pay the daycare center, whether they go or not. You can drop them off if you need to take a break.

"I'll write you out a schedule and put in some things we do when they're driving me crazy and need a distraction." She went into the bathroom.

At least she hadn't said he couldn't handle it. And why did he get the feeling she was enjoying the thought of him having all three kids by himself for days on end?

He supposed the old adage payback's a bitch was true. Hey, he was a SEAL. He could handle anything. as long as he knew he would eventually come out on the other side.

Perhaps that was what was wrong with Trish. She didn't see an end to the constant sameness of her days and nights, raising three kids by her lonesome.

While he dropped in every once in a while to be fed, clothed, cared for, and have sex. Why should she want him around when all he did was add to her workload?

He'd been ragged out from the deployment. and had slept most of the first two days at home. But after nearly a week home, now would be a good time for him to show her he was determined to pull his weight in their relationship.

CHAPTER SEVEN

THEY WENT DOWNSTAIRS for the tasting, and were directed outside to a covered patio. In the shade, the air remained gentle and caressing.

Langley counted fourteen couples who'd converged on the patio for the presentation. A tall, well-dressed woman of about thirty came out and introduced herself as Janelle Ladenburger, one of the owners of the vineyard.

"Welcome to Ladenburger Vineyards. I'll be doing a tour of the winemaking process later, around eight. But until then, I'd like to introduce you to some of our wines, and help you open your senses up to a wonderful smelling and tasting experience. Because breathing in the fragrance of the wine is as much part of processing its flavor as drinking it."

He listened carefully to her spiel about the wine having legs, which was how the liquid clung to the bowl of the glass when it was tilted. The more legs, the more alcohol it contained.

Holding a white napkin beneath the bowl she demonstrated how the color changed with the type of grape from which it was made and the age of the wine.

Then there was the body of the wine, how it felt in your mouth, and whether it was dry or sweet.

She demonstrated how to swirl it in the glass, much like he'd done upstairs in their room. She encouraged them to stick their noses into the glass and breathe in the scent to pick out the fruit, earth or spice notes of the brew.

Trish looped an arm through Langley's, and leaned in against him. Her soft breast pressed against his upper arm, and her breath brushed warm against his ear as she whispered, "You're listening so intently. Do you think there's going to be a test at the end of the presentation?"

His body quickened with need. Had she nestled up against him like that upstairs, he might have been able to persuade her not to come down for this. He'd have given it a shot. "I'm used to giving my entire attention to whoever's speaking, which right now happens to be you."

Trish's eyes fastened on his face, and maybe she read some of what he was feeling, because her cheeks pinkened for the second time today. She rocked back, but didn't release his arm or move away. Instead she buried her nose in the glass and inhaled deeply.

Langley felt some relief, knowing she wasn't entirely immune to him. Where there was a spark, there remained a possibility of igniting a blaze. He didn't mind wooing his wife. Maybe if they had to work a little to get back to where they'd been before this last deployment, it would bring them closer. That's what he wanted.

When she released his arm, he slipped it around her and rested a hand along her hip to keep her close. He studied her profile, the rounded curve of her cheekbones, and how the smattering of freckles across her nose somehow enhanced its delicate shape.

"You're supposed to be breathing in the aroma of the wine and trying to figure out what notes you smell," Trish pointed out.

"What do you smell?"

She poked her nose into the glass and closed her eyes. The delicate fan of her lashes rested against her pale skin. Her brow tightened just a hair as she concentrated. If only she'd lower that glass just a second, he might be able to steal a kiss or two.

"I smell grapes, of course, but there's a hint of black cherries, and a floral scent, like rose petals...and a little hint of caramel."

Mrs. Ladenburger slipped up next to them. "That's very

good…"

Trish's eyes flew open. She extended her hand. "Trish Marks, and this is my husband, Langley."

"It's nice to meet you both." The two women shook. "The caramel scent you smell is the oak barrels the wine has been fermented in."

"I always think certain bourbons smell like caramel. Is it aged in oak barrels too?" Trish asked.

"Yes, most of it is. You have a good nose. What do you think of the flavor of the wine?"

Trish looked into her glass. "I haven't tasted it yet. Just breathed it in."

"Try it, and let me know what you think." Mrs. Ladenburger wandered on.

Bourbon was a man's drink. Who the hell had she been around who drank bourbon? A sudden rush of jealousy made his tone a little sharp. "Since when have you been going around sniffing bourbon?"

Trish narrowed her eyes. "My dad drinks bourbon. You know that. I've always noticed the smell. I've tasted it, but it's much too strong for me."

The territorial rush eased as quickly as it arose, and he felt like an idiot.

Trish took a step away from him and withdrew her arm. "Just when do you think I'd have time to fit a man into my schedule, Langley? And what makes you think I'd even want to?"

Right now, he supposed that probably included him. His gaze drifted out into the vineyards. "Do you want to try any more wine?"

"No."

"Then I suppose we could dress for dinner."

"Yes."

He didn't attempt to touch her as they wandered back into the lobby. He set his untouched glass on the front desk, and followed Trish to the elevator. She stood back while he unlocked the door and slipped past him into the room.

"If you don't want to be here with me, Trish, just say so, and we can load up and go back home."

"That's not what I want, Langley."

"Then what is it?"

"I want something you can't give me."

He didn't have to ask what that was.

"I know I said I didn't want any more children but…" Her throat worked as she swallowed. "I can't have any more children, Langley."

Every time she said it, he felt like his feet had been kicked out from under him.

The doctors took out her uterus to save her life, and he wasn't there. He'd been out of touch for two weeks, in fact, and when he finally got to talk to her, she said she was fine.

"You should have told me when it went down, Trish."

"A SEAL's wife doesn't bother her husband with unnecessary stress while he's deployed," There was a touch of bitterness in her tone.

She set the wine glass on the dresser. "I needed you, the kids needed you, and you weren't here. I know I shouldn't be angry with you. But I am, Langley. I'm so angry.

"I could have bled to death waiting for the ambulance, and you weren't there for the children. The ambulance attendant had to ask a neighbor to come over and stay with them until the hospital could contact my mom. One of the other SEAL wives, Gloria Talbert, Lester's wife, came to stay with them until Mom could get here."

He sat on the foot of the bed, cradling his head in his hands.

"I wasn't feeling right before you left. I wasn't bouncing back. I was still bleeding from Jessica's birth."

Tears streaked her face. "I needed you. Why can't you be here just once when I need you?" She slumped onto the bed beside him.

He reached for her and held her tightly against him. "I'm here now, Trish." God, he felt so useless.

Her shoulders shook as she wept. His own eyes stung.

"I thought I was going to die, Langley, and they'd be alone, shipped off to my mom's, or yours, to grow up without either of us."

"But it didn't happen, Trish. We're both here. If anything had happened, they'd have sent me home on emergency leave to care for the children."

"Would they?" There was doubt in her expression.

"Yes, they would. If something happened to you, Trish, I'd give up the teams. I wouldn't leave them without a parent. I swear it."

She seemed to calm a little once he said that. What he did was important, it saved lives, but he wouldn't abandon his children. They had to come first. He admitted it would be a struggle for him, because he loved what he did, was driven to do it, but he'd give up everything for them.

"When I'm gone, you and the kids are the first thing I think about when I wake up, and the last thing I think about before sleep. The four of you are my talisman against all the things I have to do during my deployments. I love you, Trish. I love the kids. You have to stop keeping things from me. You have to stop carrying them alone."

She drew a deep breath and fought to regain her composure. "I don't want to distract you by dropping things on you when you're in danger. If something were to happen to you…"

Jesus, they had to stop this. "I'll make a deal with you. I'll share whatever I can when I'm downrange, and you share whatever you need to with me. This distance, this festering silence, is destroying us. If I'd known you were sick, I'd have requested emergency leave and come home, honey. I can't do anything about it now, but I'd have done whatever I had to to get home. You have to believe I would have."

Tears rolled down her cheeks, and she turned her face against his shirt. He rubbed her thin back and shoulders, offering her what comfort he could.

Trish was his rock. She didn't crumble at trouble. But this had hit her hard.

He had never been out of touch during an emergency before. But then they'd never faced a life-threatening emergency before. Everything could change forever in just a second. He knew that better than Trish. He had believed his wife and kids were insulated from that to some degree. But they weren't.

After a few moments, she seemed to regain her composure and rose to go into the bathroom. She had a wad of tissue in one hand and a wet washcloth in the other when she returned. She blew her nose.

He was relieved when she sat back down beside him. She rested her elbows on her knees and held the washcloth against her eyes, her voice muffled behind it as she said, "I'm sorry I've been a bitch to you since you got home, Langley. Sometimes things just get to be too much."

"I know." It was so hard for him to express how he felt, even to her. It was like letting a weakness show when he needed to be strong. He drew a deep breath and dove in. "When you're lying alone in bed at night, I'm doing the same somewhere else, feeling the same way, honey. There are times I want to hear your voice so much I don't think I can stand it."

"Really?" Her tear-washed eyes finally rose to his face.

"Yeah, really." He couldn't allow himself to think about those times, the close calls, and what had triggered them. He cupped her cheek. "I'm sorry I wasn't here for you, Trish."

"I know."

She finally sounded like she believed him, and he relaxed a little.

"I know the things I deal with here are nothing compared to what you deal with every day when you're away, Langley. And I know I should suck it up and move on. You'd think after nine years I'd be able to do that. There's certainly nothing I can do to change it."

Having someone close to him nearly bleed to death was exactly like some of the stuff he dealt with. If it had been him, he wasn't sure he'd be able to handle things as well as she had.

"Sometimes it's not so easy to lay down the pain, honey. I

know that. And nine years of being alone half of every year... There's nothing I can do to give you back that time, Trish." He laced his fingers, hands clasped between his knees. "Because of your job, you know better than anyone what could happen to the kids without one or both of us. That weighs on your mind."

"And it doesn't yours?" she asked.

"I've always depended on you to be there for them, Trish. I've never even imagined a world where you weren't there."

He raked his fingers through his hair. She had to imagine a world without him every time he hopped a plane and went wheels up.

The full impact of how close a call it had been for her was finally sinking in. His throat closed and he had to swallow several times. "We probably need to have a backup plan, and hope and pray it's never needed."

But he couldn't allow himself to dwell on what happened to her. If he did, he'd never be able to get farther away from her and the kids than a trip to the market.

She sounded calm when she said, "I think a backup plan would be a good idea."

"I have three more years in my enlistment, Trish. I can't just resign. But I could transfer out of the teams."

"I'm not asking you to leave your team." Her hair fell forward, obscuring her expression as she concentrated on smoothing her skirt against her leg, over and over again, in a self-soothing gesture that caught at his heart and gave it a squeeze.

She looked up. "I know how hard you've worked to get where you are, how hard you work to stay there. I know you're living your dream. I won't be responsible for your unhappiness." Her blue eyes held resolve. "And I don't expect you to be responsible for my happiness, Langley. I know I have to find it for myself."

Something in her tone hollowed his stomach. What, besides the kids, had he ever given her to make her happy? At the moment, he couldn't think of a damn thing.

She leaned forward. "Tell me one terrible moment you carry, Langley."

Saliva pooled in his mouth, and he swallowed. How could he dump such painful memories on anyone but the men he worked with, who understood? But then they never discussed what happened in combat, because so much of what they faced ended in death. If they thought too long about it, they'd have to face their own mortality.

There were memories he'd carry for the rest of my life. Things he'd never forget. Things that sometimes tormented his dreams.

"There was this young PFC, a Marine named Michaelson. His unit was attached to ours for a time. We were going into villages looking for intel on a guy, a real murderous asshole, and trying to gain cooperation from the locals so we could find him."

"Michaelson was really good. He had a natural way with the kids, was respectful of their rules surrounding women, which meant you didn't speak directly to them or even look at them, and you certainly didn't touch them. And he'd picked up enough of the local lingo to be able to communicate.

"He hung out with the kids and played ball with them. He umpired Little League games all through high school, and even had a baseball scholarship to a good college, but he enlisted instead."

"He gave us the info he picked up from the older children that panned out again and again. So we got the idea to requisition some balls and baseball bats so he could leave them behind for the kids."

He ran a hand over his face to hide his pain from her. "Bad idea. It left a trail through the villages we'd visited, and gave the terrorist assholes ideas."

"We stopped at a small village, and while we were meeting with the head men, Michaelson got his baseball thing going. He had a group of about ten kids, right in the center of the village, playing. We heard a commotion and a single gunshot. Everyone bailed out of the meeting to see what was going on.

"There were four kids down. One's arm was broken, and another's head was bleeding. The biggest one, about seventeen, was dead from a gunshot wound. Michaelson had to take him out to stop him from beating the younger kids with the bat. The other one, Michaelson had taken another bat from him and pinned him to the ground. We took that kid into custody and interrogated him, and then turned him over to the locals.

"Al Qaeda had intimidated the older boys. Threatened to kill their families if they didn't do as Al-Qaeda instructed. They told them that if we showed up, they were to attack the children Michaelson taught to play ball, because he was corrupting them with his western ideas. It was a message for the village chief and elders about cooperating with us.

"Michaelson carried the seven-year-old with the head injury back to his mother, tears streaming down his face. He had to cup his hand under the back of the kid's head because his skull was crushed. The child never saw it coming. He died in Michaelson's arms."

The mother's wails of grief cut them all like a knife. They all felt responsible for what happened, even though it was terrorist assholes responsible for that kid's death.

"It hit us pretty hard. Those of us who had kids in particular. And it pointed out to us one more time that we were dealing with people who would do anything for their cause. No sacrifice would be too much.

"The next village we went into, Michaelson refused to interact with the kids. When his unit commander tried to order him to, he told him if he did and another kid was killed, it made us no better than the terrorists, because it meant we were willing to sacrifice innocents for intel. He told the commander that if he was willing to do that, he'd have to do it himself."

"He didn't get into trouble, did he?" Trish asked.

"No. I had a talk with his commanding officer, and we agreed he had a valid point. I sent the remaining bats and balls to different units to be used for PT."

"Why would you carry this, Langley? It wasn't your fault, any more than it was Michaelson's that the little boy was killed, or the older one decided to kill him."

He remained silent for a moment. "I was the one who ordered

the balls and bats, Trish. It was my idea for Michaelson to talk the kids up."

Her features crumpled in sympathy, and she wrapped her arms around him, offering him comfort. "You couldn't have known, Langley."

He shook his head. But it didn't ease the pain or the weight of responsibility he carried, and it didn't take away the memory of that innocent seven-year-old with dusty bare feet being carried through the village by one of their men. A man who was only eighteen himself.

"Michaelson will never find joy in playing ball again, Trish. He refused to play with the other troops. Refused to even listen to a game on the radio. He'll always associate the thing he loved the most with that dead child. Because of my fucking bright idea."

And Michaelson would never forget the teenager he had to shoot.

"You can't know that. Maybe he'll find healing in it, if he'll let himself. Is he home now?"

"I don't know. I think he probably is."

"Why don't you contact him and talk to him about it? You may be able to help him and yourself, so you can both lay this down."

It wasn't how they normally dealt with things. But he might give it a shot.

CHAPTER EIGHT

THE BLACK DRESS Trish wore to dinner followed the slender contours of her body and made her skin look pale and soft. With her blond hair and blue eyes, she looked country-girl beautiful. He was aware of several of the other men in the dining room checking her out as he guided her to a table.

Whatever she'd done to tone down the blotchy look around her eyes and nose from crying had worked.

He'd never thought of his wife as fragile, but her waist seemed very narrow as he rested his hand against it. He was both concerned and aroused by this new Trish, who knocked him off-balance.

He loved her, but had taken her for granted, and she had every right to be angry with him.

But since their conversation, she seemed more relaxed with him.

The room glowed with subtle overhead lighting and lit candles on each table. Trish ordered chicken cooked with mushrooms and wine sauce, wild rice, and grilled asparagus. He ordered a medium rare steak, a salad, and a baked potato with the works.

She filled him in about families who had received orders to transfer to the East coast or Hawaii, and a couple of new babies. They talked about Tad's new obsession with robots, Anna's lack of interest in dolls, and Jess's penchant for getting up at three in the morning and playing for an hour before going back to sleep, which was largely responsible for Trish's sleep deprivation.

He drank two glasses of the red wine the waiter poured for him, and Trish seemed to enjoy the white wine they served with her meal. She shared a few bites of her chicken with him, but refused a taste of his steak, which was cooked to perfection. He signed the tab to be added to their room bill.

They went outside to walk off some of their food. He caught Trish's hand, and they walked in easy silence for a while.

She broke the silence as they paused atop the platform next to the pool that looked out over the vineyard. "I've been offered a transfer to a different department. I'd be working with at-risk families, and I'd be able to make a difference in a lot of children's lives."

It sounded like more stress and work to him. He was more worried about her taking on too much. She seemed stretched thin already.

"You know I'll always support whatever you want to do, Trish."

"It would mean more money, too."

"There are more important things than money. I'd like to see you look around for something you can feel passionate about, even if it doesn't bring in more money."

"I think this might be it, Langley."

She supported him, though he risked his life, and she'd gone through hell all alone to do it. He had no right to say a word against anything she might decide. "You could give it a shot and see if it's what you want."

"I'm still thinking it over."

At least she was including him in the discussion, which she rarely got from him. There were so many things involved with his job that cut his family completely out of the equation.

God, he was a selfish asshole, and he didn't understand at all why Trish stuck with him to begin with. All those shortcomings were being driven home at once.

"You could book a massage for tomorrow," he suggested.

"You need to take advantage of everything you can while we're here."

"I think I'll just hang out at the pool with a glass of wine. I'm beginning to like it."

Langley laughed. "The red I drank at dinner was pretty good. Are we going to go to the brewing demonstration?"

"I'd rather sit with you and talk."

That sounded both good and bad, in light of their most recent discussion.

Trish leaned into him and rested her head against his shoulder. He turned to rest back against the railing and hold her. Every month they'd been apart rose up and grabbed him, and his body responded immediately to the feel of her against him.

"I'm sorry I've been a bitch to you since you got home. I missed you, Langley. Missed the sound of you snoring as you fall asleep. Missed how you are with the children. Missed how you spoon with me while I go to sleep. Missed the way you wake me up in the mornings, kissing the back of my neck. I never stop missing you or worrying about you when you're gone."

"Thank God."

He didn't realize he'd spoken aloud until she laughed. "I feel like I'm just now beginning to understand you. In the nine years we've been married, you've never shared your thoughts and feelings with me like you have today."

He was running scared, but he couldn't admit that weakness to her. "I know you'd probably be better off if you kicked my ass to the curb and went it solo, or even found someone who's always around to share this journey with. I know you're alone too much, and I'm pretty much MIA every time you have to deal with major shit. But if you can stick it out for the next three years, I really will apply for a change of assignment, where I might possibly be home more."

"I'm not going to ask you to be someone different than you are, Langley. You'd eventually resent me for it. The person you are is who I fell in love with when we first met. But I love you for the offer. I love you for sharing your memories with me, though it hurt you to do it. It's helped me put things in perspective a little."

He rested his forehead against hers, brushed his lips against her brow, then kissed her. A surge of relief rushed through him as her lips and tongue responded to his, first with tenderness, then with a building passion. She tasted of the wine she drank with dinner and her.

Every time he returned from deployment and they kissed, touched each other, or made love the first time, it was like it was all new again. It was both familiar and precious, exciting and comfortable.

She was trembling by the time the kiss ended, and he was painfully hard.

"It's been too long, Langley," Trish murmured. "Let's go to our room."

The elevator was full of guests returning to their rooms from dinner and the winemaking demonstration. Langley tugged Trish to the stairs, and they walked up the two flights.

He scanned for cameras in the stairway, and seeing none, stopped her on the landing to kiss her again, his lips and tongue fervent. He slid his hands beneath her little black dress to cup her bottom and bring her up against him.

Trish stood on tiptoe, hooked one leg around his hip, and moved against him in a way that guaranteed he wasn't going to last long.

He groaned against the intensity of the kiss. "It's been too long for me, Trish. Nine months is a hell of a wait, honey."

"We don't have to wait any longer," she murmured against his ear, and sucked his ear lobe into her mouth at the same time she unbuckled his belt, unbuttoned his pants and slid his zipper down.

They did crazy things like this when they were younger, but not after nine years of marriage.

Her hand slid into his briefs, wrapped around his erection, and stroked. He bit back a groan, so turned on he had to visualize breaking down his M5 rifle to keep from giving in to the pleasure.

He hooked his thumbs in the sides of her panties and eased them down. Trish gave a wiggle and stepped out of them.

The sound of the door downstairs opening had them both freezing. Trish looked like a guilty teenager.

"We better go," Langley whispered.

She laughed and bent to scoop up her panties, drawing his attention to her behind. Knowing she had nothing on under that dress had another surge of desire zipping south. He'd barely gotten his pants zipped when two guests appeared on the stairs behind them.

His belt jingled as he jerked the door open for Trish, and they hustled out into the hall.

Trish laughed as he let her into their room. "I wish you'd seen your expression, Langley. It reminded me of that time I was giving you a blowjob and your mom walked in on us. I had to pretend I was looking for a lost earring under the bed."

He remembered it well. Thank God his back had been turned to the door. There wasn't a doubt in his mind his mother knew exactly what was going on, but had chosen to ignore it. "What was she going to say? We were married." He nestled up against her from behind and let her feel his erection as he gathered up the skirt of her dress and stroked her bare butt, then kneaded it.

"Oh God, it's been nine months since you've touched me like this." She rubbed against him and reached back to stroke up and down his thighs.

"You don't have to remind me, honey. I've been without you as long as you've been without me."

He bent his head to find the curve of her neck with his lips and cupped her flat belly. Trish guided his hand down over the soft hair covering her pubis. He found her with his fingertips, wet and ready. He murmured her name.

She turned against him and he found her mouth with his. Her hands got busy unfastening his pants again. His hands shook as he unzipped the dress and peeled it down. She had no bra on, and the fabric fell to the floor, leaving her naked, except for her black high heels. For the first time he saw the bright pink scar, low down on her belly between her pelvic bones, where they had cut into her and removed her uterus.

She covered the scar with her hand. Langley went to his knees, pulled her hand away and placed his lips against the mark. If they wanted more children later, they could adopt.

But they would have to talk about that when need wasn't thrumming through his entire body. The scent of her arousal made thinking impossible. He parted her and found her small, rose-blushed clit and laved it with his tongue.

Trish gripped his hair. She parted her legs more, and her hips slanted toward the touch of his tongue. "Langley—" Her voice sounded husky and weak.

After only a few moments, she backed away, kicked her shoes off, and wiggled back on the bed. Her cheeks were flushed, and he could hear her breathing, fast and unsteady. She parted her legs, exposing herself. She was glistening with moisture and deep pink with arousal. "Hurry."

He didn't have to be told twice. Trish laughed as he shucked his clothing, tossing his shirt and pants toward the dresser without looking. He crawled up on the bed and between her thighs.

She gripped him and caressed his hard length before guiding him inside her. They both made a sound—part relief, part pleasure—as he pushed inside. She tilted her hips, seating him deep, and they rocked together.

Trish cupped his face in her hands and brought his lips back to hers. "If I could hold you forever, it wouldn't be long enough, Langley."

Every time they came together after being apart, he wondered how he could have ever done without her for so many months. They both remained hollow until they filled each other up again.

His long, slow strokes were a form of familiar torture that held them on the edge. Trish's restless caresses up and down his back, her feverish kisses against his throat, his shoulder, wreaked havoc with his control.

When her breathing began to catch, he knew she was close, and the anticipation unraveled his control. That and the nip she gave his shoulder.

He pumped hard once, twice. Trish's familiar sound of release drove him over the edge, and his own climax rolled through him.

He smoothed back her hair from her cheek and kissed her again.

"Don't move yet. I just want to be close to you like this." She ran her hands up and down his back, then lower. She brushed her fingertips over his buttocks. "Remember that old movie Tad liked so much, where the guys get their clothes stolen and they run away from the lake bare-ass naked?"

"You're not supposed to talk about another man's bare ass while you're touching mine, Trish."

She laughed, her eyes alight. "No other man's ass can compare to yours, Langley, I promise." She gave his tush a light squeeze, and he started to harden again. "Tad was watching the movie again the other day, and he thinks it's the funniest thing. He made the comment that one of the men had a fuzzy butt. He wanted to know why his wasn't fuzzy."

"What did you tell him?"

"I told him when he got older he might have a fuzzy butt, too." She chuckled. "He said, 'No I won't, I'll use Daddy's electric razor and shave it off.'"

Langley snickered. "Thanks for the warning."

"You have a few years yet before you have to worry about it, I think."

She raised her hips, drawing him in deeper, and just like that, discussion of family went right out of his head.

He nuzzled her cheek, then sucked on her earlobe, and she made one of her sounds—a cross between a catch of her breath and a hum—that made him hard as a rock in a nanosecond. He cupped her breast and kneaded it.

Trish turned her head, and her mouth caught his. She no longer tasted like wine, but of her. Their lips clung again and again until he thrust his tongue forward and she sucked on it.

He thrust deep. She moved beneath him in reply, and murmured his name. He set a slow, easy pace this time, drawing their lovemaking out, pausing to kiss her, caress her, taste her skin with parted lips, and drink her in. He paused to look down into her passion-flushed face, and it was like seeing her beneath him for the first time.

It was manna, the hungry way she caressed him, kissed him, and her hips rose to take him in. She reached between their bodies to cup his balls and at the same time put pressure on the underside of his penis, so when he moved, her velvet-wet heat gripped him harder with every thrust. When he came this time, his hips jerked again and again as he spilled himself into her.

She smiled up at him and stretched, their bodies still sealed together by their release. "I'm so glad you're home, Langley."

Finally, he felt he was home.

CHAPTER NINE

CURRENT DAY, 10:00 p.m.

THE SOUND OF the alarm on one of the IV machines jerked Langley up straight in his chair, and his eyes flew open. His heart raced from the sudden sound and the lingering effect of his memories.

A nurse came in to check the machine. She flipped off the alarm. "I'll be hanging another IV bag in a moment."

Langley rose and stretched, stiff from sitting so long. He studied Trish's features. She seemed to have a little more color in her cheeks. He ran the backs of his fingers against one, just to be certain it wasn't the beginnings of a fever. Relieved to find her temperature normal, he stretched and checked the time. He needed to check on his kids.

Zoe Weaver answered the phone on the second ring. His CO's wife was a strong woman. Even with her bum leg, she just kept putting one foot in front of the other.

"How are you doing?" he asked.

"We're fine. I hung out with them, and let them talk about their mom. They've all gone to their rooms to lie down now. The girls are together in Jessica's bed."

"Is A. J. okay without you?"

"Yeah. Hawk took him home, and they're piled up in bed together. I wish him luck sleeping with him. He kicks like a mule. A.

J., not Hawk."

Langley chuckled at her attempt at humor so it wouldn't be wasted.

"Trish is still asleep, still on the ventilator," he said. "The nurse said they were keeping her sedated to give her body a chance to recover from the trauma, and because it's easier for her to tolerate the vent."

"Once she's awake, it will be her instinct to fight it. They'll probably decrease her sedation tomorrow and take it out."

He was grateful for Zoe's encouragement, but damn if it didn't make him want to tear up. He swallowed to clear his throat. "I'm going to stay here, if that's okay."

"I thought you might. Hawk's going to come over with A. J. in the morning."

"Don't forget to keep the alarm on at night. I don't know how Clarence could find out where we live, but be on your toes, just in case."

"I will. I tried to keep the kids from seeing the story on television, but Tad went online and looked it up. He printed the man's picture out and showed it to the girls and told them to watch out for him."

Langley shook his head. "You can't keep them from finding things out. I suppose it is a good idea for the kids to know what he looks like. Don't worry about it. I can't begin to thank you enough for staying with them, Zoe."

"No thanks necessary. The kids are great. And Trish would do the same for me."

She would. She was the matriarch of the wives in his team, and took the younger ones under her wing. Their group supported each other through pregnancies, illnesses, and emergencies like this one, while the men were deployed, or even when they weren't.

What would Trish do with the kids if it was him lying there?

"If you could take them to church tomorrow, so they can have something to concentrate on besides waiting to hear from me, it might be good. They can hang with their friends for a while. You don't have to stay. You can just drop them off and go back and pick them up."

"I've been attending with Trish and the kids lately, and I was going to suggest the same thing."

At least he was on the right track. "I know Trish has been shouldering a lot of things while I've been gone. I appreciate that she has you and the other women for support."

"You have your team and we have ours." Zoe's voice was husky with suppressed emotion. "The others have called to check in."

"When I know anything more, I'll call. I promise." She didn't say the kids had been asking, though he knew they would be. "You're welcome to sleep in our bed. The girls can tell you where the clean sheets are."

"Anna's given me her bed. She wants to stay close to Jessica. She's got me all taken care of."

"Okay, good. As soon as Trish is awake and able to speak, I'll call the kids."

"That would be good. They're hanging in there, but they're worried. Would you like to speak to them? I can reassure them everything is okay so they'll relax enough to sleep, but it might help to hear your voice."

"Yeah. I'll tell them goodnight."

Anna and Jessica were a little teary, but they seemed to settle down once he'd reassured them their mom was okay.

He hoped it was the truth. He wouldn't believe it fully, though, until she opened her eyes and spoke to him.

"Do you think she's still mad at me, Dad?" Tad asked, anxiety giving his voice a higher pitch.

Every moment of his behavior was probably playing over and over in his mind. A protective rush of sympathy hit Langley. "No. She doesn't hold on to things like that, Tad. Kids are expected to screw up now and then. If you didn't, we'd be out of a job. Your mother loves you no matter what."

"I'm sorry, Dad. You'll tell her I said that?"

"Yes. I'll tell her as soon as she's awake."

"She'll be okay, won't she?"

The doctor had been cautiously optimistic, but there was always a chance something might go sideways. But Trish was tough. "She's going to be just fine, Tad. I'll call in the morning when she wakes up."

"Okay."

"Help Zoe all you can."

"She's good, Dad. She's like Mom."

Nobody could be like Trish, but he understood what Tad meant. "You couldn't sweet talk her into giving you back your X-box controls?"

"I didn't even try."

"Good." He hated that his son was learning a hard lesson in a very tough way, but this would stick with him forever, and make him a better man.

As long as Trish survived.

If anything happened to her... the emotional aftermath would last a lifetime for them all.

Langley said goodnight and ended the call. He turned back to his sleeping, injured wife and wished for the thousandth time that she would open her eyes and speak to him.

CHAPTER TEN

T RISH FLOATED ON her back upon the water, the sky above her velvety dark with a scattering of stars, with a gray, wispy cloud draped around them like a scarf. The water soothed her tight muscles and made her drowsy.

The wake of someone else entering the water moved around her. She knew it had to be Langley. His fingers glided along her forearm, more a caress than just a touch. His voice was louder than she expected.

"Trish, you need to open your eyes. Come on, honey, you've slept long enough."

She obeyed him, but he wasn't alone, and she wasn't in the pool. A strange man stood beside him, and a woman. A horrible, claustrophobic feeling attacked her. She tried to swallow and couldn't. There was something in her throat, choking her. She fought the urge to gag, and couldn't resist that, either.

Langley leaned over the bed, and she focused on his face. Where was she? She reached for the trach tube, and he caught her hand. "A machine is helping you breathe for a little while. You can't touch the tube, honey."

She tugged at her hand, and an alarm on the machine started going off. She struggled against his grip.

"You have to relax, Trish. The machine is breathing for you."

She didn't believe it. She couldn't get the rhythm of it, and she felt like she was choking. Panic set in.

She gripped Langley's hand, hard, and started to sit up. The doctor placed a hand against her shoulder. The alarm continued to scream, and the doctor's voice sounded like Charlie Brown's teacher wa-wa-wa-wa-wa.

She had to breathe. She gripped the tube with her free hand and pulled it out. She heaved and coughed as she held her side where something stuck out of it. She folded in on herself in pain.

"Jesus Christ!" Langley exclaimed. He wedged himself in between Trish and the nurse and gathered her close. "Lean against me, honey. I've got you. Just breathe, slow and easy. Slow and easy, Trish."

She finally captured a rhythm that felt natural to her. She leaned into him and rested her forehead against his shoulder, trembling with reaction. His arms tightened around her.

"Raise the head of the bed." She heard the doctor's instructions clearly for the first time. "That was a dangerous thing to do, Trish. You could have damaged your vocal cords, or worse." He sounded pissed as he pressed a stethoscope against her back. He listened for what seemed forever, moving the stethoscope around from place to place.

"Now if you'll lean back so I can listen to your chest."

She felt weak and sore all over, now the adrenaline had leached from her system. She was grateful to Langley when he eased her back against the pillow.

She was finally able to see the doctor's face. He looked too young to be a physician.

He checked her throat, both with a tongue depressor, and by palpating her neck.

"Get her a cup of water," he said. The nurse poured some water from a pitcher beside the bed into a plastic cup.

Langley rose from the bed, making room for the nurse. His hands shook visibly as he raked fingers through his hair.

She held the water in her mouth for a moment to wash away the lingering stale, plastic taste before she swallowed. It hurt a little, but was bearable. She looked up to find Langley watching her every move. "I'm all right, Langley."

She sounded like she had a terrible case of laryngitis, and her chest still ached a little, but she could breathe.

While the doctor listened to her chest, the nurse wrapped a blood pressure cup around her arm and pushed the button to take a reading. The doctor folded the stethoscope around his neck. "You're moving air well, and have good breath sounds in both lungs. How would you say your pain is from one to ten?"

She assessed how she felt and held up three fingers.

"It may get worse. I'll prescribe something. And I'm scheduling respiratory therapy. They'll be here later. You'll need to exercise your lungs to keep from developing pneumonia, and to encourage healing."

He explained to her about her surgery, and how the bullet had been left in to prevent causing more damage. The longer he talked, the more tired she got.

When he and the nurse finally left, she wanted very badly to close her eyes and go back to sleep. She took a moment to really study how her body felt. A dull ache hit her every time she drew in a breath, but it was manageable.

Her throat felt dry and sore. And she felt weak, as though she'd run for miles, even though she just woke up. "More water?"

Langley poured some for her and held her propped up a bit, while she guided his hand with the cup to her mouth.

"Are the children okay?" Trish asked when she had enough water.

"They're fine, Trish. Zoe is staying with them. The girls are having fun playing with A. J., and Tad is toeing the line right now."

She nodded and relaxed a little more. "Mary Clarence and her children?"

"They're all fine. You saved Mrs. Clarence and her children's lives by calling the police. Clarence had tied them up in one of the bedrooms and brought a gas can into the house. They think it was his plan to kill them and set fire to the house."

"Who told you that?"

"One of the deputies came by to check on you, and was a little talkative when he found out I was military and a SEAL."

"So you pumped him for information?"

"Yeah." He shrugged. "I needed to know what happened."

She paused for a moment and thought back on her interaction with Clarence. "Clarence is psychotic. He accused me of trying to take his wife and children from him. Did they get him?"

"Not yet. But they're looking for him." Langley sat on the edge of the bed, grasped her hand, and absently ran his thumb over and over the back of it in a soothing gesture. Dark circles ringed his eyes, and he looked like he hadn't slept in days. His thick, dark hair stood up in disheveled whirls where he'd run his fingers through it.

She reached up and smoothed it in place. His masculine features and pronounced jaw had a homely-handsome appeal that she'd found sexy as hell when they first met. She still did. When she was better, they were going to make up for lost time. They hadn't made love nearly enough lately. She'd been too distracted by work, the children, and her own exhaustion.

"Do you think you can stay awake long enough to talk to the kids for a minute?" he asked.

"Yes."

He reached for his cell phone.

"Langley."

His attention snapped back to her face. "I love you."

His throat worked as he swallowed, and his eyes glazed with emotion. He reached for her. She went into his arms and pressed in close, listening to the strong, steady beat of his heart. Soaked in the touch of his hand as he stroked her hair.

He smelled of sweat and the hospital air, and she didn't care. Just being close to him was everything.

"I thought we were going to lose you, Trish. The kids were terrified, and I was too."

"Marshall saved my life."

"That's the deputy sheriff?" he asked.

"Yeah."

"We both owe him."

She nodded. "Clarence was going to kill me. I think when Marshall shot at him, he tripped or something. That's when the gun went off and he shot me."

Was she making excuses for the asshole? "There was blood at the scene that wasn't yours. He didn't just trip, Trish, he was hit. He would have killed you, just like he planned to kill his family. Deputy Marshall saved your life and theirs by showing up when he did."

She nodded. "I know he did." She leaned back against the raised portion of the bed, her side aching. "Call the kids. I need to talk to them."

Once she reassured the girls she was okay, they were still teary, but relieved. Anna was being brave for her little sister. "We're all fine, Mom. We even went to church this morning with Zoe and Hawk."

"That's wonderful, Anna. I hope you thanked them for taking you."

"We did."

"Good. I know I can count on you to be thoughtful like that. I love you, and I'll be home soon."

Jessica seemed a little more emotional, but quieted as soon as Trish soothed her. "Thank you for being good for Zoe, sweetheart. And I'm so glad you've enjoyed playing with A. J. You'll be big enough to babysit on your own in a few years. Think you might like that?" she asked.

"I don't know. It's pretty exhausting."

Trish held her hand to her side as laughter threatened. "Yes. Little people have a tendency to be very active. You were once like that yourself."

Jessica's, "Gee. Maybe I should apologize," threatened to trigger laughter again, and she held her breath a moment.

"You were just the way you were supposed to be, Jess. No apology necessary. I need to speak to your brother. Okay?"

"Okay. I love you, Mommy."

"Love you."

The phone sounded like it was fumbled, then breathing came on the other end. "Mom?" Tad's tone was uncertain. "You're awake?"

"Yeah. I have laryngitis, but I'm okay."

"I'm sorry, Mom."

Had he been worrying about his behavior all this time? "I know you are, honey. You're going to make everything right with Jessica, and put it all behind you. I know you are. I love you."

"I love you, too. When will you be home?"

"I don't know. As soon as the doctor says I can. But I'm better. I'm sure they won't keep me long." She glanced in Langley's direction. "I'm going to send your Dad home to get some rest. He'll be there in a little while."

"Okay."

"I need you to wake the girls in the morning to get ready for school at your regular time. Okay?"

"Yeah. I can do that."

"Thank you, Tad. It helps knowing I can depend on you to hold down the fort while we're away. I'm going to go now because I'm still very tired. I think it's the medicine they're giving me. Thank Zoe for me." She'd talk to Zoe once she was a little stronger.

"I will, Mom."

She extended the phone to Langley. "You need to go home and rest, Langley. You look really tired."

He raised his brows. "Geez, Trish. You've been awake all of forty minutes, and you're already directing the troops like a general."

She smiled. "The kids feel more secure if they stick to their regular routine. It distracts them from the situation."

"Yeah, I know. I have been known to take care of them now and then. That's why I asked Zoe to take them to church this morning, so they could hang with their friends and get out of the house." There was a bite to his tone, his jaw tense.

She bit her lip to keep from smiling. "That was a good idea."

"Thanks." He sounded only a little mollified. "You need to rest now you've talked to them."

He was right. Every ounce of energy had drained away again. "I'm turning over command to you, Senior Chief. But you need to rest, too."

"I will."

"I think I need to go back to sleep."

"I'm not surprised. You need to learn to relax a little, Trish."

"Yeah. I do. I've been going full-tilt for months."

"Don't you mean for years?" he corrected her.

She nodded. Whose fault was that? Hers? His?

And what was he going to do to help her escape this stress-laden rut she'd fallen into? Resign from the teams?

She wanted to go back to the pool she'd been drifting in before they so rudely interrupted her dream. She wanted to float on that water until she felt better. She closed her eyes with the buoyant warmth in mind. "I'm a little tired."

Langley swore beneath his breath and shook his head. "I think you need to quit your job, Trish. There are other things you can do with your degree. You could be a guidance counselor at a school, or be a geriatric advocate at a hospital or nursing home."

She counted to ten before she spoke. "You have a point, but that will be my decision. Not too many seventy- or eighty-year-old psychopaths ready to come into the hospital with a gun." Her hand gravitated to her side. "I'm sorry. I thought pulling around the corner before calling the police put me out of sight. It was a stupid move."

"I'm going to see where the nurse is with that pain medication."

Yes, the pain was intensifying, and she had a headache as well. "I think that might be good."

As soon as he disappeared out the door in search of the nurse, her eyes filled with tears. She had thought the tension between them might have been destroyed by the life-and-death struggle she'd just been through, but it hadn't. She still had to curb the need to bite his head off.

Fifteen years of being the one in charge of house and family while Langley did his duty, and lived his dream… He might have been in life and death trenches while downrange, but she was here in the trenches with their children, holding things together by her fingertips.

Then to have him waltz in and criticize her for being stressed out about it did not help. He wanted to tell her how she needed to do the job. But he had never done the job.

Maybe she needed to walk away and give him a good dose of it all. As soon as she was able to walk, she very well might do that. But could she do it to her kids?

As soon as she was strong enough, she and Langley were going to go head-to-head about some things. But right now she just needed to try and heal and get on her feet.

She needed to think of a time when things were better. Maybe that would help her feel better about the state of her marriage and family.

CHAPTER ELEVEN

SAN DIEGO, 2010

DOC AND BOWIE both paused beside the gate. Bowie gave her a hug. "Thanks for dinner, Trish." He brushed a kiss against her cheek. After he stepped back, Doc gave her a squeeze. "Good night."

Trish patted Doc's back. The two best buds and SEAL teammates wandered out to Doc's SUV and climbed inside. She watched their taillights disappear.

She loved the team. They were a great group of guys. And there was no doubt if she was in trouble, all she'd have to do is pick up the phone, and the whole team would be on her doorstep ASAP.

But there were times she felt like a frat housemother as well, since she and Langley were the only married couple in the group. Well, except for Selena and Greenback. But those two were a young married couple, and still in the "want to be alone" stages.

She remembered those times for her and Langley. It had been a while. But things were better than they were a year earlier.

She turned to track Langley's progress. Doc and Bowie had helped him put away the extra tables and most of the food. He was dragging out the last float from the pool as she approached him, and he leaned it against the privacy fence.

Something had happened during his deployment. He was still

helpful with the kids. Attentive and affectionate with her. But something was going on with him. He was quiet and moody, dwelling on something.

She caught his hand and drew him to the hammock. "The girls have crashed in their room, and Tad is asleep in front of the television. We are going to relax in the hammock before we go inside."

"We are?"

"Yes, we are."

Langley raised a brow. "How do you propose we both get into the thing without landing on our asses?"

"You jump out of airplanes thousands of feet above the ground, and you're afraid of falling two feet out of a hammock?"

He chuckled. "I thought the plan was to lie in it together, not fall out."

"You get in first. Then I'll join you."

He got in quite easily. She waited for the hammock to stop rocking before she eased in beside him. The hammock rocked wildly, and she plastered herself against Langley's large frame and held on for dear life. When it quit rocking, she gave a sigh and ran her hand up beneath his T-shirt and stroked his broad chest.

She tried to think of a way to get him to open up. "What did you think about Brett's sister, Zoe?"

"I think Hawk will try to be all noble and shit, but he won't stand a chance."

Trish laughed. "He's interested in her? How could you tell?"

"He's offered her and her mom a place to stay while Brett's situation is ironed out."

She was surprised, but then again she wasn't. Hawk had a protective streak a mile wide when it came to his men. With Brett being in a coma from a head injury… "It may be exactly what he said it was. He's just trying to help them out."

"Possibly. But he was watching her like a hawk around the other men. No pun intended."

She'd met some of the women Hawk had dated over the last couple of years. They'd all been tall, athletic, and blond. Zoe was small in stature, and had obvious mobility issues because of a permanent leg injury. But with her unusual hazelnut, sun-streaked hair and startling blue eyes, she was beautiful. "Maybe he's worried about how Brett will feel if she hooks up with one of his brothers in arms. Or maybe he's concerned she might get hurt."

Langley tucked a hand beneath the back of his head. "I think he's worried one of the guys will put the move on her before he has a chance to."

"Wow!" She remained silent for a moment, thinking that through. "What if something happens to Brett?"

"Brett's tough. He'll come through this. He's going to wake up."

She understood his refusal to accept that any of them were mortal. If they bought into it, they might lose their nerve when they needed it most. She tried to put as much confidence in her tone as he had. "I think he will, too."

Langley tightened his arm around her, giving her a squeeze.

Was he worried about something he thought he hadn't done that could have prevented Brett's injury? Was that what he was carrying? "I know there's something bothering you, Langley. Can you tell me what's going on?"

He shook his head. "Hawk and I haven't figured it out yet. I couldn't tell you even if we had, Trish."

"Okay." She continued to stroke his chest. "Tell me about something you're carrying that you can share with me."

He remained silent for a moment. "There was someone shooting RPGs across the camp fence at four o'clock every morning. It had been going on about two weeks. They managed to take out a Humvee and an empty latrine, but hadn't managed to hurt anyone.

"When the team came out of the field after that last mission, and the helo was landing, an RPG damn near hit the transport. We'd already heard that Brett was down and Hawk had an injury. Since I'd messed up my ankle and hadn't been able to go with them, it really pissed me off.

"The base commander, Captain Morrow, gave me carte

blanche to take the shooter out if I could find him. A few days later, as soon as my ankle was better, I requisitioned one of our drones. Bowie, Doc, and I took a small squad of Marines and slipped off base. I launched the drone and waited for the guy to start shooting at the base.

"I took the drone up high so I could get a fix on the location of the shooter. And we waited for like an hour, feeling like sitting ducks, because we're a convoy of four Humvees, and we're driving around in circles. Finally they fire on the base and hit a section of fence and the sandbags.

"I'm figuring out the coordinates. We move in quick to the house, prepared to take him out. The Marines bail out of the Humvees a hundred feet from the location, and I send some around back.

"We breach the front...and we find an infant in a basket who's not doing well, and a two-year-old who looks like he hasn't been fed in a while. We secure the kids in one of the rooms while we search for the shooter.

"We hear shouting from the back, and double-time it outside. The Marines have a woman on her knees in the center of the courtyard. She's begging them to kill her."

His throat worked as he swallowed. Trish put an arm around his waist and held on tight.

"We try to avoid touching the women. They're shamed if we do, and their families can shun them or kill them. But we can't not search her, because she might be wired. I do it as quickly as possible, and get the hell away from her.

"I get the interpreter over there, and we find out her husband was killed in a drone attack two months before. She and the children are completely alone. Al Qaeda has been paying her in food to shoot at the base from the roof of her house, but no one has brought her anything to eat in a week, and she's given every-thing to her son, the two-year-old. She and the infant are starving.

"The Marines are looking at me waiting for orders, so I order one to break out some MREs. We offer the woman food, but she refuses it. One of the Marines feeds the two-year-old. He's like a little bird, holding his mouth open and gobbling down the food as fast as he can. Doc gets an IV going on the baby, who's in bad shape.

"On the roof are four more grenades and the RPG. We load the weapons in one car while we load her and her kids in the other, and we take them all to the base hospital to be checked out.

"Our base commander shows up at the hospital for a sit-rep. I tell him the story. He turns to me and says, 'What do you think we should do with her?'

"He'd already given me the go-ahead to take out whoever was shooting across the base wall. I wasn't about to leave her for those Al Qaeda bastards to starve her and the kids to death, or worse. She'd done some property damage, but hadn't killed anyone. So I tell him I'll interview her and get as much information about the assholes as I can—specifically, the man who threatened her.

"I tell him I'll also take out the house, so no one else could move in and shoot at us from the roof, and then dissuade the neighbors from getting any ideas. We could possibly pay a couple of the neighbors to say the house was hit by a drone strike, so the bastards would think she and the kids were dead. And I'd relocate the mother and children somewhere else. Possibly to the husband's family, if they could be found. They'd take her in because of the children—hopefully.

"He agreed, so Doc, Bowie, Strong Man, and I go back out and wire the house to blow so there'll be a minimum of damage to the homes around it. Then we spend our last two weeks in Iraq trying to find family to send her and the kids to."

Trish's arms tightened around him again. "You're a good man, Langley."

He was silent for a long moment. "One of the Al Qaeda bastards abused her. She gave up his name right away. I think that's why she wanted to die. The baby was only about three months old. She'd given birth to her alone. And this asshole comes into her home and..." His throat worked again. "I made sure his name was on the hit list of bad guys before I left. If our guys don't get him, theirs will, maybe. Hopefully the bastard's already dead, since he never came back."

"You did all you could, Langley. More than her own people or neighbors did."

"It's damn near impossible to figure out who the bad guys are over there, Trish. Some of them would sell their kids to the highest bidder to survive, while others will stay in the trenches and starve with them. We try to build a relationship with them through kindness, and they're murdered for having contact with us, or turned in by their own neighbors. It's a no-win for everyone."

Trish cupped his cheek and looped a leg over his. "There's nothing you can do about it. And you're home. Try to lay it down."

He turned on his side, making the hammock swing wildly, and snuggled her body into his. "You're right." His mouth touched hers in the softest of kisses. "I'm home. I'm grateful to be here with you."

That's the way it always worked. He told her some non-secret something that was weighing on him, and he turned to her for comfort.

How much more did the secret stuff hurt him? How did the other guys deal with all this without a sounding board and a pair of loving arms to hold and comfort them? She smoothed his hair back from his forehead.

"I'm grateful you're who you are, Langley." She tugged up his T-shirt and then her own, so their skin could touch. He unclasped her bra and cupped her breast, then plucked at the nipple, toying with it until it beaded. Sensitive sparks trailed downward to the most intimate part of her body, and she rocked in against him, setting the hammock to swinging again.

"You know we can't make love in a hammock. I'm a SEAL, not an acrobat."

She chuckled. "I thought we could do some heavy petting, then wander in and make love." She unzipped his khaki shorts and caressed the length of his erection through his briefs while she nuzzled his neck.

"Good thing I'm a sailor and don't get seasick." He kissed her again.

She could tell he was lighter for having shared, but it wasn't the thing that was bothering him most. It was probably something he'd never be able to share. She couldn't do anything about that but love him.

SUNDAY, 3:00 p.m.

TRISH OPENED HER eyes when the nurse came in to change the IV bag. Her attention fell on the chair Langley had been sitting in. He was still there, sound asleep, with his head tilted back at an awkward angle guaranteed to give him a crick in his neck.

A wave of tenderness and love washed over her. She and Langley were better together than they ever were apart. She loved him so much. She knew she was loved in return. He tried hard to show her every chance he got.

It wasn't fair to keep riding him about things. She needed to get past this short-tempered resentment.

She didn't even know why she was so resentful and angry. What was she carrying that was causing her to feel this way? She had to figure it out and lay it down. Otherwise it was going to destroy their marriage.

His patience would only last so long. Maybe they just needed a rip-roaring fight to clear the air. But what did she want to fight with him about? Damned if she knew. She was just tired, worn down, overworked, and now she'd been shot.

Which was definitely a good enough reason to quit her job.

But Langley didn't quit his because people shot at him.

God, how stupid that sounded, to compare their jobs.

She wanted him home safe. She was terrified something would happen to him when she needed him most.

Plus the things going on between her and Tad. They both needed Langley at home to act as an intermediary. She just wasn't strong enough to make their son see he needed to take a close look at his behavior and think about the bridges he was burning.

Then why the hell was she being such a bitch to the person she needed most? Why was she pushing him away? She needed to do some soul-searching and figure it out.

CHAPTER TWELVE

FRIDAY, 10:00 a.m.

"I'M NOT REALLY supposed to be telling you this, so I'd appreciate it if you don't mention who told you," Irene said on the phone. "But I'm just so pissed off, I couldn't let them blindside you with it. And even if you come back, you'll be wondering why no one sent you cards or called."

"It's okay, Irene, I understand. I appreciate the heads-up. I won't say a word about how I found out." Trish found her hands shaking as she listened to the woman vent about their dickless boss and his idea of forcing the rest of the staff to keep their distance.

He was afraid Trish would file a lawsuit against him or the agency for unsafe work practices. He wasn't even thinking about the labor laws he broke by doubling their workload and not paying them for the many hours they worked on their own time. He knew they were all conscientious, and would continue to do the job for the people depending on them, even if they wouldn't be caught dead doing it for him.

And God knew it wasn't for the money.

"It isn't right, but there's not anything we can do about it, Trish. We can't walk off the job and leave our people high and dry." Irene's voice shook, and she sounded close to tears.

"I don't expect you to fight my battles for me, Irene. I think you've shown character just by making this phone call, so don't worry about it anymore. Okay?" She felt a bit like crying herself. That fucker had turned his back on her instead of looking out for her.

"I'm sorry." Irene said for the tenth time.

"It isn't your job to apologize for Fletcher being an asshole, Irene. But he'll do it to my face when I come back to work."

"So you're coming back?"

Trish wasn't sure, but she'd go back one last time to tell him face-to-face to stuff it, just on principle. "I'll be back soon. In the meantime, if you could check on a couple of my cases."

They spent the remainder of the conversation on the particulars of two children who'd just been placed in a foster home, and a woman who was recently evicted from her apartment because they were tearing the place down. She'd waited too long, or perhaps just hadn't had the money to move. Trish had placed her and her baby daughter temporarily, but the woman and baby needed something permanent.

After they discussed the particulars, Irene went on for another few minutes, apologizing again. "I'll take care of these people. Don't worry. And come back whenever you feel up to it."

"Thanks, Irene. I appreciate it."

Trish ended the call and leaned back to relax and bring her blood pressure back down. She could feel it pounding in her ears.

After all the years she worked for that asshole...After all the extra hours she put in that she could have been spending with her family...Fletcher could go fuck himself. He deserved to have an attorney pay him a visit, just to scare the shit out of him.

Langley wandered in from making a trip to the car with the clothing and other things that had accumulated in the past five days. Even sick, she couldn't just sit and watch television. It drove her crazy. So she'd caught up on some reading and finished some case notes.

Langley studied her features, and even reached over to touch her cheek. "You're not running a fever, are you?"

"No." She wasn't ready to tell him. It could wait until she

caught her breath and thought it through. And maybe talked to a lawyer. She wasn't about to let her asshole boss spoil the pleasure of leaving this place.

"I'm just excited about going home. I've missed the kids, missed our bed, missed having you cuddle up to me until we go sleep...among other things."

He grinned. "Glad to know I'm good for something."

"There are several things you are very good at."

"Don't go there until the doc tells you it's okay to go there."

Trish chuckled. "I'm not promising anything."

Langley's smile stretched into a grin. "I'll go tell the nurse you're ready to leave."

"I'm very ready."

IT FELT STRANGE leaving the insulated safety of the hospital. Trish stepped off the tram in the parking lot, Langley hovering within a hand's reach as they walked the short distance to the car. It was her car. The car she'd been sitting in when Clarence... She remembered every moment of the encounter.

And she'd been shot because a clerical error at the jail released him from custody by mistake. She wanted to go down to the jail and kick someone's ass.

Langley hit the button on his key fob to unlock the doors. "How you doin', hon?"

"I'm okay." The words were automatic. But she wasn't doing okay.

Langley opened the car door for her. "Doc and Bowie ran over and picked up your car. I was worried it would be towed if we left it parked there for very long."

"That was good." She slid reluctantly into the passenger seat.

Langley walked around and got in behind the wheel. Trish's gaze ran past him to the driver's side window.

"What is it, Trish?"

Her mouth was dry, and her breathing was coming in quick

gulps. "He pushed the barrel of the gun to the window and threatened to shoot me through the glass if I didn't open the door."

Langley reached for her hand. "I'm sorry, honey. I should have thought…"

"Remember that promise you made me a few years ago, about putting in for a transfer to a different MOS, Langley?"

"Yeah."

"You have one more enlistment before your twenty. I'll quit my job, if you promise me you'll do it. I want you closer to home the last enlistment. I need you closer to home." She heard the plea in her voice, and swallowed it back.

"I'm up for promotion, and Hawk's mentioned he wants me on his staff. If the promotion comes through, I'll be doing something different."

"If the promotion comes through."

"Yeah."

She swallowed again, and tried to think clearly enough to work through what a promotion would mean for him. "You deserve it, Langley. You've put in the time and the effort."

"I've been doing extra things to gear up for it, Trish. On deployment and off. It will come through."

She didn't want to ask what those extra things were. They risked their lives so often. He'd earned two silver stars and four bronze stars for his service. And he'd never mentioned what he did to earn them. No particulars of the mission.

Emotion nearly overwhelmed her. She beat it back. "I hope so, and I really want you to have it. Tad will be starting college in five years. He may decide to follow in your footsteps."

"I'd be proud if he did, but I'd rather he go to college and explore other options first. As an engineer or computer analyst, he can serve as a civilian and get paid like an officer. Or even enlist and earn a starting rank of ensign."

"You should have gone to officer candidate school and become an officer. You're smart, well-trained, disciplined. We held you back when you were younger."

"Do you think I regret that, Trish?" He brought her hand to his lips. "We have three great kids, and I have you, and you've been through it all with me. I love what I do. But, because I'm older, and have more years of experience, I've gotten to lead missions, and do things others might not have experienced until they were in the teams a lot longer. I wouldn't change a moment of it."

Her heart lifted, and she started to get teary, but smiled instead. "We might never have gotten to live in Hawaii if you hadn't enlisted."

"That's true." He eyed her. "Now, about quitting your job...I never realized how dangerous these home visits could be until this happened, Trish."

"They aren't, ninety-nine percent of the time. But when children are being removed from the home, it's an emotional minefield."

"Or when there are abusive, psychotic assholes involved."

She nodded. "That, too. But above and beyond the money, I have to say sitting home drawing unemployment with nothing to do but housework doesn't appeal to me."

Langley laughed. "It boggles the mind even thinking of you sitting still for five minutes, let alone being home alone for that long."

"It would drive me crazy."

"You have some time to heal, and to think it over."

She nodded. He was trying to be supportive and non-judgmental. She had to give him that. The more rest she got, the less resentful she felt.

"You don't have to be superwoman. You don't get paid for working on Saturday. You're going to have to grow some calluses on that tender heart of yours, and think of yourself a little more."

"It's hard to think of yourself when there are children being neglected, abused, or going hungry, Langley. I'm always afraid I'll miss something, or let it slide, and something horrible will happen."

"Have you ever thought how much alike our jobs are?"

"Yeah. We're both driven to serve. We're both trying to protect other people who can't protect themselves. We're spending time away from our kids that we could be spending with them. And lately people are shooting at us both."

His throat worked as he swallowed. "You have been giving it a great deal of thought."

She looked away. Tears rose up to clog her throat and dim her vision. "I know you can't quit this close to retirement. I don't expect you to. It isn't you I have an issue with, or even your job. Truly, it's not. You're just handy to catch the shit I dish out when I'm upset."

She looked up. "I'm angry that I've spent so many years of my life doing this job, and haven't even received a get-well card from my boss, or a phone call to check on me."

"He's an asshole. I told you that the first time I met him. Don't let it get to you."

She nodded. "I'm not going to. I just want to see my kids and sleep in my own bed."

"Roger that." Langley started the car.

LANGLEY JOGGED AROUND the car to stand close by while Trish got out. They had brought two of their three children home from the hospital to this house. He could read the relief in the relaxation of her features and the small smile that curved her mouth.

Watchful of her progress as she walked to the front door, he stayed within grabbing distance. It had been a long five days, but she made it through with good grace after that first day.

And now she was home.

He scanned the street for any strange cars parked nearby. Clarence was still at large. An edgy uneasiness had plagued him since the beginning. He wouldn't relax until that man was behind bars. Or dead. Where the hell was the guy? Why the hell hadn't they found him?

They climbed the three steps to the porch, and she waited for him to unlock the door. The house was quiet except for the sound of music playing from down the hall, possibly in Tad's room.

She scanned the room. "Wow. Did some of the girls come over and clean house for me?"

The furniture shone, the hardwood floor was sparkling clean, and the hall and the area rug had been vacuumed.

"Nope. The kids did it. They've been taking on some chores while you were in the hospital."

"Great! I'll have to thank them."

"I thought it could be a permanent addition to their chore list. I upped their allowance a couple of bucks apiece."

Trish remained silent a moment. "What's going on, Langley?"

"The kids and I had a long talk, and we decided we've been taking you for granted. We've been sitting on our asses, letting you do the lion's share of the work while we reap the benefits. So we're all turning over a new leaf."

He pointed toward the kitchen. "They're probably out back on the deck doing something to celebrate your homecoming. Why don't you have a seat, and I'll go out and see what's going on."

"Okay." She let him get to the doorway before she said his name. He turned to face her. "How long do you think this will last?"

"At least a week. Maybe."

Trish laughed. "I appreciate the effort, and where it's coming from."

"I appreciate the fact that you keep me around when I fly through here between deployments. I don't know what I'd do, where I'd go, if you didn't, Trish. I'd be lost without you."

He continued, though she started to tear up. "I'm so glad you're home, and the kids will be, too. I've worked their asses off this week."

She laughed while she brushed tears from her cheeks.

After Trish settled in the living room, he double-timed through the freshly-cleaned kitchen and out the back door. The kids were sitting at the picnic table with the babysitter, Melissa, a teenager from down the street.

Something in their posture struck him as soon as he stepped out the door.

Jessica was cuddled up to Anna, her eyes red from crying. Melissa had her arms wrapped around the two girls. Tad's back was turned to him. He didn't turn to face him, even when he walked up to the table.

If Tad had done something...

The small cake the girls had spent all morning baking was half gone. "What's going on, guys?" Tad jerked when he laid his hand on his shoulder, and half turned. One eye was swollen shut, and a large reddish-purple bruise encompassed the area around it. Shock reverberated through him. "Jesus, Tad. What happened?"

"He mouthed off to me, trying to be a big man, and got what he deserved." A voice came from the corner of the house where the deck angled back to the privacy fence. "We've been waiting for you and your wife to get home."

Langley turned to face the man who'd spoken. His gaze brushed over the guy's face, but snagged on the gun pointed at him.

Langley assessed the gun first. A twenty-two revolver. He could see the bullets in the cylinder. He could see two chambers were empty, which meant there were at least four more rounds in the pistol.

The man behind the gun was about five foot nine, and a hundred and forty-five pounds. His hair, thinning on top and cropped close to his head, appeared more gray than brown.

His eyes were dark, and gleamed with the promise of more violence. Langley had seen that look in more than this guy's eyes.

A tattoo of a snake spread along the guy's forearm, and his face was beaded with sweat. A piece of sweatshirt, gray with grime and brown with old blood, banded his upper arm.

"Where's your wife?" he demanded. The barrel of the revolver jerked with every word.

He was too worked up. This guy might shoot someone by accident. He wasn't going to get another crack at Trish. "Her lung collapsed after you shot her. The doctor decided he wanted to do another X-ray and some kind of breathing test before she left to come home. So I came on without her."

Clarence's eyes narrowed and his mouth compressed. "You're lying."

Langley kept his voice level. "No I'm not. We were all packed to come home. All her stuff is in the car. She's going to call me when they're done."

"I want to know what they've done with my wife. Call her."

"The police have relocated her and the children. Trish won't know where she is, and they won't give out that information."

Clarence's face flushed red and he stepped out from behind the house. "You better hope they will. Call. Her."

Having a gun pointed at him didn't unnerve him the way it would have Trish or the children. But if the man shot at him and missed, he might hit one of the kids. If he could just get the guy close enough, he could disarm him.

Langley removed his phone from his shirt pocket. "What instructions do you want me to give her?"

"Tell her to call her office and find out where my wife and kids are. Make up some kind of excuse to talk to them. Tell her to tell my wife to call your number."

Would they be able to hear Trish's phone inside the house? He hoped not. He dialed her number and waited for her to pick up.

"Are the kids doing something out there?"

"No, honey. Thomas Clarence is here." He left off 'he's armed.' "He wants to know where his wife and children are."

She remained silent for a long moment, her breathing choppy. "Are the kids all right?"

He wouldn't mention Tad's eye. It was just a bruise. *Please God, let it be just a bruise.* If the eye was damaged... He cut off the thoughts. He had to stay focused and wait for an opportunity to disarm this guy, or take him out. "Yes, they're all right."

"Does he know I'm here?"

"No."

"The police won't give out any information."

"He wants to speak to her, on my phone."

"Oh, God." Her breathing got more ragged. "I'll call Marshall and see if someone will forward a message."

"Okay."

"I'll call you back."

"Okay."

He closed the phone and looked up at Clarence. "She's making some calls to try and get in contact with your wife."

Langley didn't hold out much hope for that. The police would never go for it, and once they learned this was a hostage situation, they'd converge on the house like locusts, and probably get them all killed. They might allow his wife to talk to him, but if they charged the house…

"Can I get some ice for my son's eye?" Langley asked. He pointed to a small dorm refrigerator tucked within a cabinet with a slate countertop. The grill was at the end. Barbecue forks, tongs, and spatulas hung off a towel bar next to the grill. He eyed them for their utility as weapons.

"He can get his own ice."

"Go ahead, Tad." He gave his son's shoulder a reassuring squeeze. "Get the ice and put it in a plastic bag, top right drawer of the cabinet."

As soon as Tad made the ice pack and sat down again, Clarence's attention returned to Langley.

"Lay your phone on the table and get into the pool." Clarence used the gun to motion Langley toward the water behind him.

Langley's attention settled on the children.

Maybe this guy was smarter than he seemed. Or maybe he intended to kill him now he'd made the phone call. A man who planned to kill his own family and set fire to their house wouldn't think twice about shooting him in front of his children.

"How did you find our house?" Langley asked, hoping to distract him.

"I watched your car, and followed the guys who drove it here."

Jesus. If he'd just left the damn car where it was…

"Your son said you're some big, bad Navy SEAL. I heard you guys like the water. You can show me how well you swim."

Thomas Clarence wasn't interested in his swimming technique. He was planning to neutralize a threat.

CHAPTER THIRTEEN

TRISH'S BREATHING CAME in gasps while she dialed Marshall's number. She slipped through the kitchen and stood to one side of the sliding glass door to peek out. Clarence was holding a gun on Langley, and Langley was backing toward the pool.

Ashley held the girls as close as her arms would reach, but they were all frozen with fear, their faces pale. Tad came into her range of vision. He held a bag filled with ice pressed against his left eye.

What had that fucker done to her kid? Fear and rage rushed through her, filling her ears with static. Her whole world was out there with a psychopath.

Marshall's voice dragged her back from the edge. "Trish, how are you?"

"He's here, Marshall. Clarence is here at my house, and he's armed. He's got my kids and husband out by the pool at gunpoint. He doesn't know I'm here. He wants to speak to his wife. He wants her to call him back on my husband's number."

"What's the address, Trish?"

She rattled off her address.

"What's the phone number?"

She was beginning to calm down, until she looked outside and saw Langley pulling off his tennis shoes, socks, and shirt, and getting into the water. God, it had to be cold. Too cold to swim in.

"He's forcing Langley to get into the pool." She spoke the fear that was raging through her. "Oh, God, he's going to kill him."

That asshole was not taking her husband from her. He was not taking her family. She hung up and laid the phone on the counter. It immediately began to ring again. She ignored it. Langley's gun safe was locked, and she didn't have a key. Why didn't she have a key?

She strode through the living room and down the hall to Tad's room. It had never looked so clean or organized. She spoke aloud to the empty room. "Please don't tell me you moved your bat."

The Louisville Slugger had been propped in the corner next to the dresser for months, and she sighed with relief when she saw it was still there. She'd helped Tad practice his stance and swing for hours. They'd even gone to a batting cage near Old Town to practice.

Bat in hand and her resolve set, she rushed back down the hall to the kitchen again. Langley stood in the pool up to his waist. Clarence stood over him, gun raised and pointed at her husband.

Langley backed away from the man and pushed off the bottom of the pool with a smooth lunge. She'd seen him swim up and down the pool for sometimes an hour without a break. Her heart hitched as he hit his stroke and started digging deep, his kicks powerful and sure. Clarence tracked him with the gun.

Trish took off her shoes, slid the door open about a foot, slipped through the narrow space, and, careful not to hit the frame, brought the bat out behind her. She took her eyes off of Clarence long enough to check the kids. Jessica's face crumpled as she saw her, and tears ran down her face, but she didn't move. Trish raised a hand praying they'd all remain still. She padded across the deck and down the steps, her focus on the back of Clarence's head.

Fifteen feet away, she noticed the angle of her shadow. She'd have to rush at him so he wouldn't see her coming.

"Faster," Clarence yelled. She jerked and caught her breath.

Langley suddenly changed course and cut diagonally across

the pool swimming toward Clarence, his arms punching the water like a boxer.

The phone on the table rang. Clarence's body tensed, his grip on the gun shifting as he tried to divide his attention between Langley in the pool and the phone.

Trish broke into a run, lifting the bat over her shoulder. She planted her feet. One second. Two.

The gun jumped in Clarence's hand.

Trish swung with all her might.

The crack of the wood striking his head was like a limb breaking off a tree. Clarence's whole body jerked sideways, and he dropped, his limbs loose. He hit the concrete with a dull thud and lay still. The gun skittered across the concrete and flipped into the pool.

Instant nausea hit Trish and she gripped her knees.

Langley surfaced and climbed out of the pool, blood streaming down his leg, along with the water that ran from his soaked shorts.

"Mom," Tad was beside her within a second.

At the first close look at his eye, her stomach rolled again. She swallowed against the nausea. She couldn't fall apart. She had to deal with Langley's injury first. She handed the bat to Tad and pointed at Clarence. "If that man as much as twitches, hit him again, and don't hold back."

The phone continued to ring. She ignored it and turned to Langley. "Where are you hit?"

"Jesus Christ, Trish. He could have killed you," Langley complained.

"You're fucking bleeding, Langley. Where are you hit?"

He looked down at the puddle of blood and water at his feet. "I don't know."

"Looks like it's coming from your back. Turn around so I can see." He did as she asked, and she bit her lip. There was a hole in his pants over his right buttock.

The babysitter, Ashley, rushed forward with the girls. She looked pale, but seemed composed as she handed the phone to her. "It's an Officer Marshall."

Trish took the phone, but pointed to the cabinet next to the grill. "Get me some towels from that cabinet over there." She dragged Anna and Jessica close to her. "Go in the house and wait for me there. I have to help Daddy."

Suddenly her composure slipped, and her eyes flooded with tears.

Langley laid a hand on her shoulder, "Take it easy, Trish. I think I'm okay. It doesn't even hurt. It may just be a nick."

Trish put the phone to her ear. "We need two ambulances. Langley's been shot, and Clarence is down. I may have killed him. With a baseball bat." Her voice shook, and she shuddered.

Tad glanced up from his guard duty. "He's still breathing, Mom."

She spoke into the phone. "You'd better hurry."

His TEAM STOOD around the bed, seven men who had pulled his ass out of the fire too many times to count, just as he'd done a time or two for them. They were all a little bewildered about why they'd been left out of the fight.

"Jesus, man. Why didn't Trish call us?" Bowie asked, his tone midway between outrage and befuddlement. His dark brows met in a deep V at his straight blade of a nose.

The throb in Langley's backside was a painful heartbeat, and he was grateful when the nurse appeared. She was about his age, a little thick around the waist, with ash blond hair and a sweet smile. She took a syringe from her pocket, removed the cap, plunged a needle into the IV line plugged into his right arm and emptied the medication into the system. "That ought to make you more comfortable, Senior Chief."

"Thanks." It took only a moment for the meds hit his system. The pain eased to a dull twinge.

She nodded. "Five minutes, gentlemen," she said to the rest of the room. "Senior Chief Marks needs his rest."

As soon as she left the room, Langley formulated an answer. "There was no way anyone could reach us in time, Bowie. We walked into the house, and the kids weren't there.

"When I left they were baking a cake to celebrate Trish's homecoming, so I thought maybe they were setting something up outside on the deck to welcome her home.

"I walked out, and the next thing I knew I had a guy pointing a gun at me from the corner of the house.

"He'd already smacked Tad around, bruised his face and blacked his eye. And he'd terrorized the girls and the babysitter by putting a gun to their heads.

"He wanted Trish. He already tried to kill her once. I couldn't call her out there and give her to him. I told him they'd kept her at the hospital for a few more last-minute tests before releasing her.

"He wanted to speak to his wife, but he was going to take us all out. He had four rounds left in the gun. One for me, three for the kids, and he could drown the other one in the pool."

He swallowed as the aftermath of what could have happened threatened to overwhelm him.

"I called Trish, told her what he wanted, then tried talking to him to get him to come closer, but he kept his distance and forced me into the pool. He told me to swim laps, and kept the gun trained on me. But I saw her sneak outside with the bat."

He shook his head.

"She doesn't spank the kids. She doesn't ever raise her voice, not even to me, when she's mad, but she was going to try and take him out alone. I thought he'd see her coming, thought he'd shoot her before she reached him. The bastard had already nearly taken her from us. She'd just gotten out of the hospital, and I wasn't sure she'd be strong enough to take him down."

He started getting emotional again and took a deep breath. "I started swimming toward him as hard and fast as I could, to distract him and draw his fire." His throat worked. "Tad said she swung the bat like Clarence's head was a ball and she was aiming for the lights. The bastard went sideways and down.

"Then she went into protective mom and wife mode. I didn't

even know I was hit until she said, 'You're fucking bleeding, Langley. Where are you hit?'"

"Jesus!" Hawk breathed. His Native American features had never looked more chiseled. "You never know what you're capable of until someone is threatening someone you love. Trish did you proud, keeping it together like that, and facing someone who'd damn near killed her. But if that fucker dies, she'll need to talk to someone, Langley. What we do prepares us, but she's never raised her hand to harm anyone before. In fact, the total opposite."

Langley hadn't thought about that. "We'll deal with it. I promise. Whatever she and the kids need."

The nurse popped back in the room.

"It's time for us to move out, guys," Hawk said. He offered his hand to Langley. "Trish and you have our number. Whatever you need."

"Thanks for everything, Hawk." Langley met his gaze for a moment. "I'll be back up and running long before we need to go wheels up again."

Hawk nodded.

The rest of the guys lined up for a fist bump, even the new guys, Sizemore, Tyler, Logan, and Masters. Greenback and Bowie hung back to the last. They slapped his shoulder and gripped his hand.

"Who needs us when you have Trish?" Bowie said. "If I ever find one like her, I might be tempted to settle down."

"If she was anything like Trish, you'd be lucky if she'd have you," Langley countered with a grin.

"Selena and I are there for you, Bro," Greenback said. "You guys or the kids need anything, you have our number."

The nurse held the door for them, and bustled back in after they left. "They seem like a good group of guys," she commented as she hooked him up to a blood pressure cup.

His emotions high, he nodded silently, giving himself a chance to settle again. "The very best."

After the nurse left, he rolled gingerly onto his left side and closed his eyes. The painkillers she'd given him took the edge off his aching ass and made him drowsy.

How ironic that he had been through so many deployments without a scratch, only to come home and get shot in the ass. As soon as he was feeling better, he knew the team would start giving him crap about it. It would be just too good to pass up.

Fingers brushed his hair back from his forehead, and he opened his eyes to look up at Trish. She was still a little pale, but she smiled.

What was a little nick in the butt if it kept her and the kids safe?

She bent close to rest her check against his. "Are you flying high, sailor?"

"No, but I have a nice buzz going."

She smiled. "How would you like some company?"

Langley grinned. "Sure."

She dropped her purse in the chair next to the bed and wiggled up on the mattress. He looped an arm over her hip to pull her in close on the small bed.

He asked about the one thing he'd been worrying about more than himself. "How's Tad's eye?"

"The ophthalmologist said it's going to be okay."

His breath whooshed out on a sigh of relief.

"Good. I'm relieved. Where are the kids?"

"Believe it or not, Bowie volunteered to take them out for ice cream. He thought doing something normal after all this might help them shrug some of it off. He's going to drop them off at the house in an hour or so."

Langley grinned. "You have at least half an hour before you have to leave to get back to the house. Want to mess around?"

"They must have put something more than pain meds in that IV, Langley. You're wounded." Worry shadowed her blue eyes.

"Darlin', I don't feel a thing."

"You turned and swam toward him to draw Clarence's fire, didn't you?"

Langley grasped her hand and placed it against his cheek. "I was the threat. I'm a man, bigger and stronger than him, and trained to take out terrorists. I had hoped I could get him close enough to take him down. But once I went into the water, it wasn't an option. When you came out of the house, I knew you were our only chance. So I gave him the target he wanted, and gave you an opportunity to take him down."

"Oh, God, Langley." She gripped the hospital gown they'd given him to wear and burrowed her face against his chest. Her shoulders shook as she sobbed. After a few minutes, she dragged her composure back around her and wiped her face with a corner of the sheet. Her voice sounded thick with emotion when she said, "You could have been killed."

"It was a small-caliber weapon, and I was hoping he wouldn't hit anything important."

"God, you're such an idiot. There isn't a single inch of your body that isn't important to me—to us."

"The same goes for you and the kids, honey. I did what I had to do to give us all a chance."

"Yes, you did."

"You put your life on the line for us, too. And for Thomas Clarence's wife and children. Clarence is going to live, and he'll go to jail for a long, long time—for kidnapping, assault, attempted murder, and half a dozen other things. His wife will never have to worry about him again, and neither will we."

His arms tightened around her, his fingers gently brushing along the nape of her neck, and she relaxed beneath his touch. "They're going to kick me out of here in the morning. I don't think a flesh wound calls for any longer than that. I only have a few stitches."

"You'll have a dimple on your butt," she said with a small laugh.

"Something I've always wanted."

"A badge of courage."

He refused to allow her to move things in that direction. "Right on my ass."

"It will be sexy as hell."

"I'm glad to know you think so, since you'll be the only woman to see it."

Her eyes held the shimmer of tears as she brushed the back of her fingers against his jaw. "You're my hero, Langley Marks. My lover, my husband, my everything."

Shit, she got him with that one. It was either kiss her or embarrass himself by crying. He moved in for the kiss and her lips were warm and responsive. When he came up for air, he murmured, "And you're mine, Trish."

EPILOGUE

6 MONTHS LATER, 2017

TRISH BUCKLED THE strap on her sandal and rose to smooth the fabric of her skirt. She turned to take a look at Langley in his dress white uniform. He looked sexy as hell. He didn't get to wear it nearly enough, in her opinion. There was really something about a man in uniform….

Langley looked up from studying his white shoes and smiled. "What are you thinking about?" he asked, sidling up to her and looping an arm around her waist.

"You know exactly what I'm thinking about." She ran her fingers over the ribbon bars that covered the left side of his uniform jacket beneath his SEAL Trident. "Think we could talk someone into to taking the kids, so we can come back here and I can peel you out of this uniform."

A grin stretched across his face. "I'll ask around as soon as I get there." He bent his head and kissed her, setting off the familiar chain reaction of galloping heart and tingling heat between her legs.

"If we had time…" There was a promise in his hazel eyes.

"But we don't, and if we don't get a move on, you're going to be late for your own ceremony. But you have a date later, regardless."

"Sounds good."

"Hey, Mom," Tad wandered into the room, breaking the mood.

Trish bit back a sigh.

"Can you tie this for me?" He flipped his tie up and down. "I keep getting it too long in the back."

She stepped in front of him and realized she was looking him directly in the eye. When had he grown another two inches? She quickly tied his tie and smoothed it down. When he gave her a hug she returned it fiercely.

"We have to get a move on, guys," Langley said.

Anna and Jessica were in the living room, dressed and ready to go. Jessica grabbed the camera off the coffee table as she stood. "I can take pictures, can't I, Daddy?"

"Sure, honey. Just don't post them online, okay?"

"I won't."

Langley herded everyone out to the car and took his place behind the wheel.

As they merged onto the 1-5, Trish dwelled on how much better a place they were in now as a family. Though she hadn't found the perfect job yet, she was still looking. At least she'd had a month's leave before returning to her old one.

Family counseling had made all the difference to their recovery, and it helped the children put their episode with Thomas Clarence behind them.

Though Langley couldn't join them there very often because of his training schedule, he seemed to have benefited from it. Or maybe he'd benefited from her being less stressed.

As though reading her mind, he grasped her hand and gave it a squeeze. He continued to hold her hand until he had to exit the I-5 to merge onto a different freeway.

Her stomach fluttered with nerves as they crossed the bridge onto Coronado. After fifteen years of hard work, Langley was about to achieve one of his goals. Emotion clogged her throat, and she turned to look over the seat at the kids so he wouldn't notice.

Tad was listening to his MP3 player and looking out the window, ear buds in his ears. Jessica flipped through some of the pictures she'd taken in the past few days, and Annaliese gazed out the window, her expression distant, a book lying in her lap, something that was as common as breathing. They were growing up, becoming more independent by the day.

Langley swung into the parking lot outside one of the office buildings. He threw the car into park and cut the engine. "All right, team. Admiral Parks will be here to observe the ceremony, so be on your best behavior."

Annaliese spoke for them all. "We will, Daddy."

"Thanks, Annabelle." Langley exited the car.

The team had already arrived, and were clustered on one side of the conference room, close to the food tables. "I'll be back in a minute." Langley wandered off to join them while Trish got the kids settled.

Zoe Weaver and Selena Shaker joined her, and they hugged.

"Are you nervous for Langley?" Zoe asked.

"Yes. It started in the car, and hasn't let up since." Trish pressed a hand to her midriff.

"I'll be the same for Oliver. He's up for promotion now. Bowie is, too."

"They'll make it." Trish laid a hand on Selena's shoulder. "This was the best team Langley's ever been associated with. The guys who have moved on are all excellent leaders. Hawk did an amazing job with everyone." She left off Derrick Armstrong on purpose.

Trish took a seat next to the kids, with Zoe and Selena on the other side of her. They talked about the kids and the possibility of another deployment looming.

Her attention wandered around the room. An effort had been made to decorate, and make the conference room look more festive. White tablecloths with red, white, and blue streamers twisted together draped the tables. The shallow platform at one end of the room had the flag displayed, and a small table holding the medals and ribbons to be given out.

Trish's gaze snagged on a tall officer bearing down on them, and automatically stood, along with the other two women. Ribbons covered his chest in an awe-inspiring display. His gray hair and brows looked pale against his skin, and deep crags carved into his cheeks like dimples. As he smiled, they added to his charm.

"Good afternoon, ladies. I'm Admiral Max Parks." He shook hands with each of them, and waited for them to introduce themselves. "I wonder if I might borrow Mrs. Marks for a moment?"

At Zoe's and Selena's, "Sure" and "Certainly," he guided Trish aside, a short distance away.

Nerves whipped through her system, making her short of breath.

"I've been hearing good things about you, Mrs. Marks. Captain Jackson happened to mention the incident at your home last year. I hope everyone has recovered from the trauma now."

"Yes, we're doing fine."

"James—Captain Jackson—also said you and your husband often open your home to your husband's team. He also mentioned in particular how you take the new military wives of some of our SEALs under your wing and show them the ropes. And that you've built a relationship with many of them."

"I do what I can. I'm friends with quite a few. It's difficult to fill out all the paperwork for things when you're new to the process. If their husband deploys before everything is signed, it throws the family into a no-man's-land for those services. It helps to have someone who's been around the block a few times to help them get squared away. We have a support team to help each other out when things happen while our husbands are gone."

"He also mentioned you were a family services social worker."

"Yes, sir. I've been doing it for thirteen years."

"So you're used to juggling several cases at a time."

"Yes. More than several. Although I'm not at liberty to say how many." Where on earth was this going?

He nodded. "Would you be interested in leaving that position?"

Shock held her immobile for a second. "I've been looking for another job off and on for the past three months, but I haven't found a good fit yet."

"I'm aware of a position that's available. It's a program for retired and disabled SEALs, to ensure their needs are met. I thought, with your ties to the SEAL community, your husband being on active duty, and your background, you'd be perfect for the position. You'd be a supervisor to caseworker investigations, and direct services where they're needed. I took the liberty of calling the director and inquiring about the particulars, and he faxed some information about the job and an application to my office." He removed a folded envelope from his pants pocket and offered it to her.

Overwhelmed, Trish automatically accepted the envelope. She bit her lip and focused on the envelope until she was certain of her composure. "Thank you, Admiral. I appreciate this."

"We need someone in that position who cares about our men."

"Yes, sir. Thank you." She offered her hand again, and he shook it warmly.

"I have to go and call things to order. Captain Jackson had planned to do this presentation, but was called away. So I'm stepping into his shoes. Congratulations on your husband's promotion and commendation."

"Thank you, sir."

She stared at the envelope, but looked up as she noticed a ring of white shoes surrounding her.

"What did Admiral Parks have to say?" Langley asked, his expression alive with curiosity. Bowie and Greenback, along with Hawk and two other members of the team, weren't hiding their curiosity very well either.

"You guys are so nosy," she teased.

"C'mon, Babe. Dish," Bowie said, using his pet name for her, since her run-in with Thomas Clarence. At least the guys waited until Clarence recovered from his injuries and accepted a plea deal on all the charges before adopting the nickname of Babe, as in

Babe Ruth, for her.

"He was encouraging me to apply for a job at a program for retired and disabled SEALs. He even brought me an application."

"That's…amazing, Trish," Langley laid a hand on her shoulder. "If he's already spoken to someone there, you'll be a shoo-in if you want it."

"I'll have to see what it's all about before I apply."

"If everyone will take their seats, we'll get started," Admiral Parks announced.

Langley brushed her cheek with his lips and headed for his seat, just in front of where she and the kids were sitting with Zoe and Selena. His team took a seat surrounding them.

Admiral Parks began. "When a man decides to become a SEAL, he doesn't do it alone. His family is there with him every step of the way. I want the family members who are here today to know we are grateful for your support. Our men couldn't do it without you. And thank you for being here today to celebrate their accomplishments."

"If Senior Chief Langley Marks will rise and come forward."

Langley rose and strode up to the raised platform. Trish was aware of movement around her, and glanced to either side. Every man around them had his phone in hand and had risen to leave. She saw Langley reach the Admiral and salute, then glance over his shoulder at Hawk.

Hawk signaled five minutes, and he leaned forward to say something to the Admiral. Zoe and Selena slipped out the door with the team.

"Senior Chief Langley Marks, you have been promoted to Master Chief." The Admiral handed him the insignia he would normally have pinned to Langley's collar during the ceremony. "Congratulations. Also, for your gallantry in battle during a mission in Africa the twenty-first day of October of last year, I award you the Silver Star."

They exchanged a handshake, and Langley double-timed it off the stage. Her stomach in knots, Trish rose and signaled the children to move with her to the aisle. They stepped outside into the hall as a family, where Hawk and Greenback were saying their good-byes.

Langley turned to face them. "I have to go." He handed Trish the boxes with his medal and insignias.

Trish swallowed against the knot in her throat. "We know." She tucked the boxes in her purse. If she cried, it would get the girls upset, and she wouldn't have Langley upset because he'd left them in tears. She drew a deep breath and girded herself to wait until she was alone to give in the emotion building in her.

Langley knelt to bring the girls in close. "I love you. I'll be back as soon as I can." He kissed each one of them.

"Can I take your picture in your uniform, Daddy?" Jessica asked.

"Sure, honey." He rose and took a step back so she could snap the picture.

"Tad." He beckoned to him. He bent his head as he spoke quietly to his son. Tad nodded, and Langley drew him in close to hold him for a moment. "Love you."

"Love you too, Dad."

He turned to Trish. "Check out that job, it sounds promising." He unbuttoned his uniform jacket and handed it off to Trish.

She draped it over her arm. "Yeah, it does, and I will check it out."

He cupped her face in his hands. "I love you."

With her arms full, she couldn't hold him as close as she wanted to, but her lips clung to his when he kissed her. "Be careful. Come home soon."

"Will do." He brushed his lips across her forehead, and paused a moment to look into her eyes. She saw the love and reassurance he offered her. Trish hung on to her composure by an eyelash.

"Langley, we need to go," Hawk called out, already moving down the hall toward the exit.

"Coming."

Her voice came out thick with emotion. "I love you, Langley. And we're so proud of you."

He kissed her again. "I have to go." He took two steps to follow Hawk, then turned back. "I need a rain check on that date."

Trish's heart swelled, and she laughed. "You've got it. I'll be waiting."

His long strides took him around a bend in the hall all too quickly.

Zoe and Selena fell into step with them as they followed the route the men had taken to exit the building.

"Mom, if you and Daddy are married, how can you still date?" Annaliese asked.

Trish smiled as she thought about it.

She and Langley had never stopped dating. He, the decorated SEAL, was the romantic in their relationship, and she the practical one.

Maybe that was why they stayed bound to each other, despite separations and disagreements, good times and bad.

She adored the romantic man who gave her cornhusk flowers, and took her on romantic getaways, and asked for a rain check on a date with his wife.

"That's a good question, Anna. Why don't you ask your father when he comes home and see what he says?"

THE END

BOOKS BY TERESA J. REASOR

MILITARY ROMANTIC SUSPENSE:
Breaking Free (Book 1 of the SEAL TEAM Heartbreakers)
Breaking Through (Book 2 of the SEAL TEAM Heartbreakers)
Breaking Away (Book 3 of the SEAL TEAM Heartbreakers)
Breaking Ties: A SEAL Team Heartbreakers Novella
Building Ties (Book 4 of the SEAL TEAM Heartbreakers)
Breaking Boundaries (Book 5 of the SEAL TEAM Heartbreakers)
Breaking Out (Book 6 of the SEAL TEAM Heartbreakers)
Breaking Point: A SEAL Team Heartbreakers Novella
Breaking Hearts (Book 7 of the SEAL TEAM Heartbreakers)
coming soon

PARANORMAL/URBAN FANTASY ROMANCE:
Timeless
Whisper In My Ear
Deep Within The Shadows

HISTORICAL ROMANCE:
Highland Moonlight
Captive Hearts
To Capture A Highlander's Heart: The Wedding Night
(A Highland Moonlight Spinoff Novel)
To Capture A Highlander's Heart: The Trilogy
(all three parts of the Highland Moonlight spinoff series in one book)
Print and ebook

SHORT STORIES:
To Capture A Highlander's Heart: The Beginning
(A Highland Moonlight Spinoff)
An Automated Death (A Steampunk Short Story) Paranormal
Caught In The Act (A Humorous Short Story) Contemporary Romance

NOVELLAS:
To Capture A Highlander's Heart: The Courtship
(A Highland Moonlight Spinoff)
Have Wand, Will Travel
(A Magic and Mayhem Novella)
Have Wand, Will Travel: Once Bitten, Twice Shy
(A Magic and Mayhem Novella) Coming June 2017

CHILDREN'S BOOK:
Willy C. Sparks: The Dragon Who Lost His Fire

ANTHOLOGIES HER WORK IS BEEN INCLUDED IN:
SEALed With A Kiss: Heroes With A Heart (Breaking Free)